RACE FOR FREEDOM

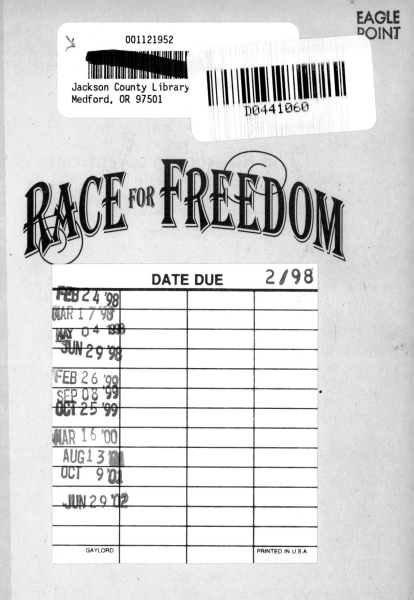

DATE DUE		2/98
FEB 24 '98		
MAR 17 '98		
MAY 04 1998		
JUN 29 '98		
FEB 26 '99		
SEP 08 '99		
OCT 25 '99		
MAR 16 '00		
AUG 13		
OCT 9 '01		
JUN 29 '02		
GAYLORD		PRINTED IN U.S.A

The Riverboat Adventures

1. *Escape Into the Night*
2. *Race for Freedom*

Adventures of the Northwoods

1. *The Disappearing Stranger*
2. *The Hidden Message*
3. *The Creeping Shadows*
4. *The Vanishing Footprints*
5. *Trouble at Wild River*
6. *The Mysterious Hideaway*
7. *Grandpa's Stolen Treasure*
8. *The Runaway Clown*
9. *Mystery of the Missing Map*
10. *Disaster on Windy Hill*

RACE FOR FREEDOM

LOIS WALFRID JOHNSON

BETHANY HOUSE PUBLISHERS
MINNEAPOLIS, MINNESOTA 55438

Published by Bethany House Publishers
A Ministry of Bethany Fellowship, Inc.
11300 Hampshire Avenue South
Minneapolis, Minnesota 55438

Printed in the United States of America.

Library of Congress Cataloging-in-Publication Data

Johnson, Lois Walfrid.
    Race for freedom / by Lois Walfrid Johnson
        p. cm. — (The riverboat adventures ; #2)
    Summary: In 1857, while helping to conceal a runaway slave on her
father's Mississippi River steamboat, twelve-year-old Libby looks to God
for support and hopes that her friend Caleb will let her join the
Underground Railroad.
    ISBN 1–55661–352–0
    [1. Underground railroad—Fiction. 2. Slavery—Fiction.
3. Steamboats—Fiction. 4. Mississippi River—Fiction. 5. Christian
life—Fiction.] I. Title. II. Series: Johnson, Lois Walfrid. Riverboat
adventures ; #2.
PZ7.J63255Rac   1996
[Fic]—dc20   96–4433
                                                                 CIP
                                                                  AC

*To Betty
and to
Chuck and Lori,
my courageous,
filled-with-fun friends*

Contents

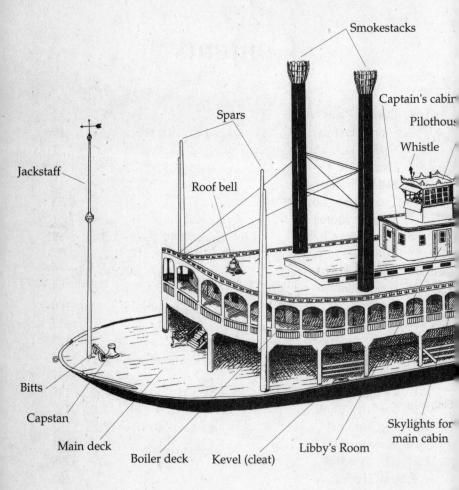

Smokestacks

Captain's cabin

Pilothous

Whistle

Spars

Roof bell

Jackstaff

Bitts

Capstan

Main deck

Boiler deck

Kevel (cleat)

Libby's Room

Skylights for
main cabin

The Side-wheeler
Christina

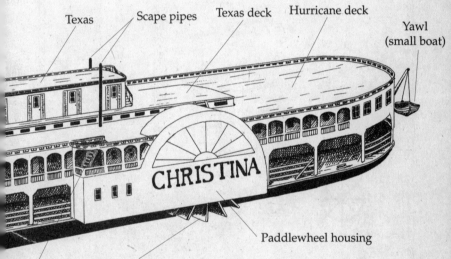

Texas   Scape pipes   Texas deck   Hurricane deck   Yawl (small boat)

CHRISTINA

Paddlewheel housing

Stairway   Paddlewheel

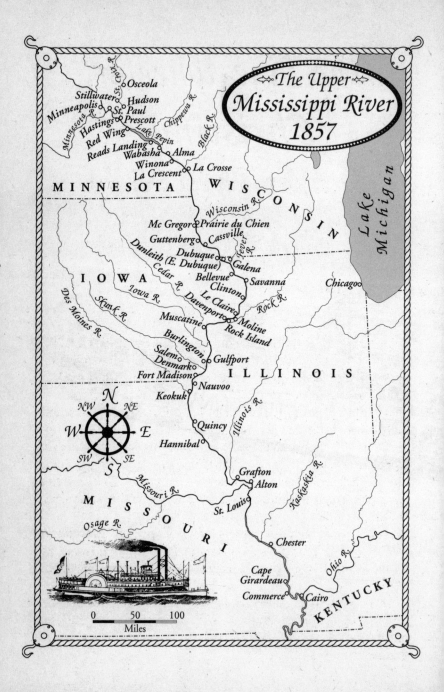

The Upper Mississippi River 1857

Osceola
Stillwater
Minneapolis
St. Paul
Hudson
Prescott
Hastings
Red Wing
Reads Landing
Wabasha
Alma
Winona
La Crescent
La Crosse

St. Croix R.
Minnesota R.
Chippewa R.
Lake Pepin
Black R.

MINNESOTA
WISCONSIN

Wisconsin R.

Mc Gregor
Prairie du Chien
Guttenberg
Cassville
Dunleith
Dubuque
(E. Dubuque)
Galena
Bellevue
Savanna
Clinton
Le Claire
Davenport
Muscatine
Moline
Rock Island

Fever R.
Rock R.

Chicago

Lake Michigan

IOWA

Des Moines R.
SKunk R.
Iowa R.
Cedar R.

Burlington
Salem
Denmark
Gulfport
Fort Madison
Nauvoo
Keokuk

ILLINOIS

Illinois R.

N
NW · NE
W · E
SW · SE
S

Quincy
Hannibal

Grafton
Alton

Kaskaskia R.

MISSOURI

Missouri R.
Osage R.

St. Louis

Chester

Ohio R.

Cape Girardeau
Commerce
Cairo

KENTUCKY

0   50   100
Miles

1

Darker Than Night

A lantern hung near the gangplank, casting a glow over the *Christina*'s deck. Libby Norstad's deep brown eyes sparkled in its light. "We got away!" she whispered to Caleb. "We really got away!"

To Libby it seemed a miracle. For the past two days and nights, they had faced constant danger.

Caleb Whitney's blond hair fell over his forehead, nearly reaching his eyes. He grinned at Libby, then glanced up at the hills of Burlington, Iowa. The steamboat owned by Libby's father lay at the landing. While deckhands brought in the gangplank, Caleb kept watch.

Now, late at night, the streets looked empty, yet Libby knew that Caleb was searching for someone. Near the riverfront, the windows of tall warehouses seemed like dark eyes staring down at them.

With three quick blasts of the whistle, the *Christina* put out into the Mississippi River. As the strip of water between the land and boat grew wide, Libby felt relieved. In spite of all kinds of danger, they had escaped!

Just then Libby felt a movement behind her. As she turned, she saw Jordan Parker creeping forward without a sound. When he drew close to the lantern, he stopped, as if afraid to enter the circle of light.

A fugitive slave, Jordan had managed to get away from his master, a cruel slave trader named Riggs. Like Caleb, Jordan also stared up at the city. On the streets above them no one stirred. Then a dark shape stepped out from the shadow of a warehouse.

Jordan moaned. "It's Riggs!"

With one quick movement, Caleb lifted the glass of the lantern and blew out the flame. Libby dropped down on her hands and knees, but it was too late.

"Riggs knows," she whispered as Caleb joined her behind piles of freight. "He saw you."

"He saw you too," Caleb warned, his voice low.

A feeling of dread tightened Libby's stomach. "What should we do?"

Caleb shushed her. "Sound carries on water."

A short distance out from shore, the *Christina* started to turn. As her bow swung around to face downstream, Libby stared at the man next to the warehouse. Then the center of the boat blocked her view.

"How long was Riggs there?" she whispered. "How much did he see?"

"Too much," Caleb told her. At thirteen, he was a year older than Libby. Now Caleb led her and Jordan to a place at the front of the boat where no one could hear them talk.

When the boys dropped down on crates, Libby found a nail keg to sit on. "You're sure it was Riggs?" she asked. It had been too dark to see the man's face, and she wanted to believe they were wrong. According to Caleb, Riggs was the cruelest man he knew.

"It were Riggs, all right." Jordan's voice held no doubt. "He gots one shape—and I knows it!"

"But he could have stayed hidden," Libby answered. "Why did he step out so we could see him?"

"That man *wants* us to know he's on our trail," Jordan said.

"He wants to scare us any way he can."

In the darkness Libby shivered. As long as the slave trader searched for him, Jordan would never be safe. Libby didn't like being frightened by the sight of Riggs, but deep inside she trembled just thinking about him.

Then she remembered. "Jordan, you weren't in the light. Maybe Riggs doesn't know that you're with us."

Jordan sighed. "I wish you was right, Libby. That man Riggs is like a bloodhound on my trail. When he sniffs out Caleb, he sniffs out me."

Since the age of nine, Caleb had worked on the Underground Railroad, the secret plan to help runaway slaves reach freedom. Once fugitives started on the secret route, they usually kept moving if it was safe. Instead, for special reasons Jordan would stay on the *Christina*.

"What's wrong?" Caleb asked Libby, as though sensing her worry.

"N-n-nothing!" Libby hated the sound of her voice. "Nothing at all!" If she told Caleb what bothered her, he would think she was a scaredy-cat. Instead, Libby tried to push her fear away. *I want to have courage*, she thought. *Courage like Caleb and Jordan.*

On that March night in 1857, Libby knew the penalty to anyone who helped runaway slaves on their race to freedom. According to law, slave hunters could follow fugitives into free states. There they could gather a posse and bring runaways back to their owners.

Leaning closer, Caleb peered into Libby's face. When she tried to hide her feelings, the light of the moon gave her away. "You're scared," Caleb said. "You're scared that Riggs will come on board and find Jordan."

"Well, doesn't that frighten you?" Libby asked.

"Nope," Caleb answered.

"What do you mean, *nope*? Pa is captain of this boat and owner too. Don't you care that he could be arrested for hiding a runaway slave?"

"Of course I care!"

"You don't sound like it!" Libby felt upset now. "You know what would happen if Riggs found Jordan on the *Christina*. It's the law of the land that Pa could be found guilty for hiding a fugitive. He'd have to pay a big fine!"

"Is that all you're worried about?" Caleb asked. "The fines? The money?"

Libby stared at him. "What if Pa can't pay the fines? He would lose the *Christina*!"

"Yup! He would." Caleb didn't sound too upset.

"What's worse, Pa could go to jail! Wouldn't you be scared if the captain were your father?"

Caleb sat with his back to the moon. Darkness shadowed his face, but Libby saw the shake of his head. "There's something that bothers me a whole lot more," he said.

"What's that?" Libby asked. More than once she had found it hard to understand this strange boy. "What could be worse than Pa going to jail?"

Before Caleb could answer, Jordan leaped up. "Don't you worry none," he told Libby. "First stop we make, I leaves the boat."

"No!" Caleb exclaimed. "Don't listen to Libby! You can't leave now!"

"Yes, I can. I ain't goin' to hurt Libby's Pa."

"That's true," Caleb answered. "You aren't going to hurt Captain Norstad."

"But you heard Libby."

"Yup, I heard." Caleb sounded angry. "And I won't let you hurt her pa. I'll keep hiding you for as long as you need to be hid."

Jordan shook his bowed head. "I was wrong to ask Captain Norstad if I could stay."

"He gave his permission," Caleb answered. "Remember?"

"I remembers. And he gave me a job." Jordan's shoulders shifted as though the idea of working for pay gave him pleasure.

"Don't forget the reason Captain Norstad said you could stay."

Jordan straightened. " 'Cause I wants to find my daddy. I wants to be my momma's hands. Momma is mighty strong. But if she runs away, she ain't got enough hands for my sisters and my brother."

In the moonlight Jordan stood sure and tall. "Momma don't know if I is dead or alive. She be moanin' and weepin' for me, and here I is—free as a bird from a cage!"

For the first time since seeing Riggs, Jordan's gaze met Caleb's. "When I leaves this boat, I is goin' to the place where Momma lives. I is goin' to help my momma and my sisters and my brother escape!"

"You want to go there *now*?" Caleb stared at Jordan. "You can't do that! On every tree and building, there are posters about you! Every slave catcher on earth wants to collect that big reward!"

But Jordan was wearing his proud look—the look that reminded Libby of royalty. With his head high, he spoke. "When I was just a little boy, my momma told me, 'Jordan, you is goin' to lead your people to the Promised Land. You is goin' to take them to *freedom*!' "

"That's right," Caleb answered. "You *will* lead your people to freedom! But if you try now, you'll lose *your* freedom."

When Jordan blinked, Caleb rushed on. "Have you got a plan figured out? Do you know a way to disguise who you are?"

Jordan shook his head.

"Do you know how to get to where your mother is?"

Again Jordan shook his head. "I ain't never seen where Momma lives now. When I gits there, I'll know what to do."

"Then let's think of a way you can get there without being caught," Caleb said.

Looking as though he didn't want to listen, Jordan dropped back down on a crate. "We gots to figure out that plan real soon," he said. "I ain't goin' to wait for something more to happen to Momma."

As if Libby were no longer there, Caleb leaned forward, speaking to Jordan. "I want to help you find every member of your family. You tell me what to do, and I'll do it."

"I tell *you* what to do?" Again Jordan leaped to his feet. This time his eyes blazed. "You is foolin' me, sure enough! There ain't no slave boy who tells a white boy what to do!"

"I know what to do if I find a runaway slave," Caleb said. "I know how to hide a fugitive who comes near the *Christina*. What you need to do will be a whole lot harder."

Standing as still as a stone, Jordan seemed to consider Caleb's words. Finally he turned. "You thinks I can lead my people to freedom?"

Caleb's gaze held steady. "I *know* you can lead your people to freedom. If you'd like my help, you've got it." As though wanting to shake on it, Caleb offered his hand.

Jordan stared down at Caleb's hand, then looked up. "You *really* wants to help me?" he asked.

"I really want to help you," Caleb said.

As if he had never before touched a white boy's hand, Jordan hesitated. Then, seeming to make up his mind, he stretched out his own hand. Halfway between the two boys, their hands met.

Jordan grinned. "I hope you knows what you is doing."

"First we keep you safe," Caleb promised. "Then we figure out a way to get to your family."

In that moment Libby felt scared right down to her toes. Something important had been decided. Something that would change Jordan's life, but also Caleb's and hers. Even the thought of what might happen frightened Libby.

I wish I had their courage, she told herself again. Then she remembered the man on the Burlington street. It had been too dark to see the evil lines in his face. Yet a shiver of fear ran through Libby—a shiver so strong that she trembled.

With all her heart, she wanted Jordan's mother and sisters and brother to reach freedom. With all her heart, she wanted Jordan to find the father who had been sold away from the family. But Libby knew how dangerous it would be.

One idea haunted her. *How can we hide from Riggs wherever we go?*

As if knowing her thoughts, Caleb spoke. "We can be sure of one thing. Riggs will do everything he can to stop us. Wherever we are, he won't be far behind!"

2

More Mystery

*I*n spite of her fear, Libby remembered. Helping fugitive slaves was something she believed in. Before she
could change her mind, Libby spoke up. "I want to help."

"No!" Caleb's answer sounded like an explosion.

Libby tossed her red curls. "I want to be a conductor on the
Underground Railroad! I want to help runaway slaves reach
freedom."

"And I said *no*. You're not getting into it!"

"You let me help the last time," Libby pleaded. "I did what
you wanted, and you know it!"

Caleb paid no attention. "We let you help because we didn't
have any choice. Just because you did something once doesn't
mean you'll do it again!"

But Libby would not back down. "You think I'm a scaredy-
cat, Caleb Whitney. I'm not! I'll do what you tell me."

"Good." Caleb stood up. "Right now I'm telling you to keep
out of Jordan's business and keep out of mine. Then we'll get
along just fine." Without another word he started away.

"Caleb?" Libby called after him, forgetting that someone

might hear. "What could be worse than Pa going to jail?"

Caleb kept going. "C'mon, Jordan," he said.

"You tell me, Caleb Whitney!"

No answer came from the darkness. Already they were gone.

I'll show them! Libby told herself. With quick tugs she pulled off her shoes. Walking on silent cat feet, she hurried after the boys.

In the moonlight she watched them find a pathway between the freight and passengers crowding the main deck. At the door of the engine room, Caleb looked around.

Quickly Libby stepped back into a shadow. After a moment she peered out. Both boys were gone.

They're in the engine room, Libby thought, once again following without a sound. When she reached the door, she opened it quietly and stepped inside.

Off in the corner, a lantern glowed. Libby walked toward the light. Halfway across the room, she heard something behind her.

Stepping aside, she ducked into a hollow between machinery. For three or four minutes, she waited and saw no movement. At last she moved on again.

Suddenly a voice leaped out of the darkness. "Looking for something?"

Filled with terror, Libby yelped. "Caleb Whitney!"

Libby's heart pounded with fright. Turning around, she fled. As she passed out of the engine room, she slammed the door and raced for the stairway at the front of the boat.

The *Christina* was four decks high. From the main deck, Libby flew up a flight of stairs to the boiler deck, then up another stairway to the hurricane deck. From there it was only a few more steps to the texas deck and Libby's own room.

Standing outside the door, she drew a deep breath. "Caleb Whitney, how could you?" she exclaimed. "Just because you're Pa's cabin boy! Just because Pa trusts you more than most people! How can you be so mean?"

Libby drew a deep breath. "I will *never* follow you again!"

In that moment Libby realized she was talking out loud. She

also understood something else. *That's probably exactly what Caleb wants! That I don't follow him!*

Lifting her head, Libby tossed her red curls. *I'll show him! Caleb is not going to scare me off!*

From the darkness Libby heard a soft woof. Ignoring Samson, her big Newfoundland dog, she took the stairs to the pilothouse two at a time. Samson followed close behind.

While a young girl, Libby had often visited this small room at the top of the steamboat. Then her mother died, and Libby had stayed with her aunt in Chicago during four long years. Only a few weeks ago, Libby had come to live with her father on the *Christina*.

As she opened the door to the pilothouse, Samson squeezed his way through. The pilot stood with his back to Libby at one side of the great wheel he used to steer the boat. Because of its size, part of the wheel went down through the floor.

Turning toward Libby, Mr. Fletcher lifted his hand in greeting. As he looked back to the river, Libby moved forward. Standing out of the way, she gazed down beyond the bow of the steamboat.

Ahead of them the great Mississippi River spread wide on both sides of the *Christina*. Libby breathed deeply and let the excitement she always felt flow into her. All her feeling for the river seemed to center here in the pilothouse.

For as long as Libby could remember, she had loved the mighty waters, the shape of trees along the shore, the islands midstream. Always she had liked to travel, to see new places and things. On the river there was always something exciting around every bend.

Yet Libby's fears also centered here in the pilothouse . Steamboats exploded, caught fire, struck the hidden roots of old trees, and sank within minutes. Whenever Libby heard about a steamboat accident, she felt unwilling to face the idea that something could hurt Pa. *No!* she told herself. *Nothing will happen to him!*

In spite of that fear, Libby liked being with her father on the *Christina*. She had pushed her worries aside, believing that Pa could keep her safe. Having Jordan on board would bring a new kind of danger.

Riggs will know where we are! Libby remembered again. *All he has to do is find the* Christina *going upriver or down. And sooner or later, we'll come into St. Louis where Riggs lives.*

Libby's stomach tightened into an uneasy knot. *When I know what Riggs might do, how can I possibly have courage?*

As though sensing her thoughts, Samson pushed close. His wagging tail thumped against her leg. Bending down, Libby ran her fingers through his coat of long, black hair. When Samson's tongue reached out to lick her hand, Libby dropped to her knees and threw her arms around his neck.

When Libby stood up again, she felt strangely comforted. Yet the knot in her stomach was still there.

※

The next morning Libby entered the captain's cabin at the front of the texas deck. Each weekday she and Caleb met here for their school lessons. On one side of the room was Pa's bed. The rest of the cabin served as a sitting room and place to bring guests.

Libby's father sat in his large rocking chair. On the floor next to him lay a pile of newspapers. Bold letters across the top page told Libby he was reading the *Daily Hawk-Eye & Telegraph.* He must have picked up the papers in Burlington.

"Hi, Pa," Libby said.

His long arm reached out, circling her waist. Yet to Libby's surprise, Pa's gaze never left the newspaper.

"Are you reading about Lake Pepin?" she asked.

Each spring steamboat captains waited eagerly for the ice to move out of the lake and the opening of riverboat traffic to St. Paul. That meant an exciting race between steamboats.

Captain Norstad shook his head. Still without looking up, he said, "Just catching up on the news."

Standing beside him, Libby watched her father. Even sitting down, he looked tall and slender. Except for the touch of white above his ears, his wavy black hair was as dark as his captain's uniform. As he held up the newspaper, one of his hands trembled.

"What is it, Pa?" Libby asked.

When Captain Norstad put down the paper, he looked up at her. Tears stood in the dark brown eyes so much like Libby's.

Fear tightened her throat. "What's wrong, Pa?" Not since her mother died had she seen her father so upset.

Just then Caleb entered the room. After one look at the captain, he sat down at the table without speaking.

Captain Norstad pushed back his chair and stood up. "How could they?" he asked. His tears were gone now, replaced by anger. "How could the Supreme Court of the United States make such a decision?"

Pa waved a hand at the newspapers on the floor. "There are several articles about the Dred Scott decision. But look at this one!" He slid a paper across the table. "It explains how I feel."

Filled with curiosity, Libby looked over Caleb's shoulder, but she didn't understand what the articles said. "What are they talking about?" she asked finally.

Captain Norstad explained. "Dred Scott is a slave who has lived in a free state and a free territory. Based on that, he asked for his freedom. The Supreme Court ruled that because he's a slave, Dred Scott is not a citizen of the United States. According to them, he has never been free because he's personal property."

Captain Norstad shook his head in disbelief. When he sat down again, he showed Caleb the place where he had marked each newspaper. "We need to study all of this," he said. "A lot of people are going to be upset about this ruling. It could lead our country to war."

"To *war*?" Libby asked. War was even more frightful than her other fears. "How could America go to war?"

Just then Libby heard a soft thump outside the cabin. As she glanced toward a window, she wondered if she saw a quick movement. If someone had been there, he was already gone.

Maybe I imagined it, Libby thought and turned her attention back to Pa. With Libby and Caleb sitting at the large table, Captain Norstad began teaching the day's lessons. Libby tried to keep her mind on what he said. Yet she noticed when Jordan looked through the window in the upper half of the door. So did Pa.

"Come in," he called.

With a captain's uniform over one arm, Jordan walked to a closet and hung up the jacket. Instead of leaving again, he found a broom and started to sweep. Often he turned his head as though listening to what the captain said.

Libby wondered about it. Both Jordan and Caleb worked as cabin boys. Had Jordan come in now because he wanted to know what was going on?

"I have a number of short trips delivering freight in Iowa and Illinois," the captain told Libby and Caleb as he gave them their assignment for the next day. "We'll go up and down this part of the river for a few weeks before returning to St. Louis. When we get there, I want you to visit the courtroom where Dred Scott made his first try for freedom."

When Captain Norstad went out, Libby and Caleb stayed to study. In the midst of her reading, Libby looked up. Still holding his broom, Jordan leaned over the table, looking down at the newspaper. From there he moved on to Pa's large map of the Mississippi River. With one finger Jordan traced the river downstream.

Soon Libby realized that Caleb was also watching Jordan. "Want to see where we are?" Caleb asked.

When Jordan nodded, Caleb turned the map to give him a better look. "Here's Burlington, Iowa, where we were last night. During the night, we passed Keokuk and Fort Madison, Iowa. In a few minutes, we'll come to Quincy on the Illinois side of the river."

Caleb's finger pointed to the opposite bank. "After that we'll stop at Hannibal, Missouri."

Jordan's gaze followed Caleb's finger as it moved on down to

St. Louis. Finally Jordan grinned. "Now I wants to show you something."

Without another word, Caleb followed Jordan out of the cabin. When the door closed behind them, Libby leaped from her chair. Outside, the boys clattered down the stairs to the deck below. Libby waited as long as she dared, then followed them.

Soon Caleb and Jordan disappeared on what was called the boiler deck because it was just above the boilers. Looking this way and that, Libby tried to catch sight of the boys. *I've lost them!* she thought frantically.

Not knowing what else to do, she hurried toward the bow and down the steps to the main deck. There Libby caught sight of Caleb rounding a corner.

They're headed for the engine room again! Libby hurried after them. *What's going on there?*

Unwilling to be caught a second time, she passed into the cargo area at the center of the boat. From there, she entered the engine room by a different door.

Ahead of Libby lay one of the large boilers that heated water and created steam to run the *Christina.* Yet Libby saw only the men who usually worked there. *Strange,* she thought. *I was only a minute behind Caleb and Jordan.*

Wasting no time, Libby walked through the engine room to the other door. When she found it tightly closed, she felt confused. The room was noisy, yet she had heard no opening or closing of doors. *I'm sure that Caleb and Jordan came in here. Where did they go?*

Puzzled, Libby tried to think it through. *How did they manage to hide from me?*

3

Search Warrant!

$\mathcal{I}$n the days that followed, Libby trailed the boys more than once. Each time they disappeared somewhere near the engine room. When that happened, it made Libby even more curious. *What's their big secret? Why won't they let me in on it?*

Finally Libby asked Caleb, "Are you still watching for Riggs?"

"Yup," he answered. "Aren't you?"

Libby nodded. "I'm starting to wonder if I'll recognize him."

"You will," Caleb told her. "Remember the deep lines from his nose to the outer corners of his lips? It's like he does nothing but frown."

Libby remembered all right, though she wanted to push aside all thought of Riggs. She wanted to forget the danger to Jordan and Pa, but Caleb's words stayed with her: *"We can be sure of one thing. Wherever we are, Riggs won't be far behind!"*

Then one April morning, Libby woke to the crowing of a rooster. In her room high on the texas deck, Libby lay in bed, listening to the sounds of a great city.

During the night the *Christina* had come into St. Louis. On the cobblestone levee, wagons rumbled and horses clip-clopped. Farther away, blacksmiths pounded their hammers.

Libby slipped out of bed and poured water into a basin. Quickly she splashed her face and dressed.

Libby's room was seven or eight feet wide and six feet long. It had two doors, one on either side of the boat. A window filled the upper half of each door. To give privacy, shutters closed outside the doors.

Opening the shutter on one side, Libby looked across the mighty Mississippi River. Just then the great orange sun edged up over the horizon. When it grew too bright to watch, Libby turned to the opposite door. From there she looked toward the city of St. Louis. Tall, new buildings stood in a proud row near the levee. The rising sun caught the stones and brick, turning the buildings pink.

The city drew Libby. She wished the *Christina* could stay in St. Louis for a long time. She wanted to see all that was going on in this important gateway to the West.

Already workers filled the levee. Up and down the gangplanks they scurried like ants bringing food to a nest. Wherever Libby looked, barrels and crates waited to be loaded onto a steamboat.

When Libby heard the bawling of oxen, she wondered about the trail that drew countless pioneers westward. Then all other thoughts flew out of Libby's head. Striding across the levee was a short, slender man.

Libby stared at him. *Well dressed,* she thought. *Expensive-looking suit in the latest style. A fashionable cane with gold on the handle.* From the way the man marched straight toward the *Christina,* he didn't need the cane for walking.

Six or seven other men followed behind the first. With each bold step they took, Libby's dread grew. When the first man was close enough for her to see the evil lines in his face, she felt certain. It was Riggs!

Forgetting her shoes, Libby hurried out on the texas deck. Only a few steps below lay the hurricane deck. From there Libby looked down. A clerk stood next to the *Christina*'s gangplank. When Riggs handed him a piece of paper, the clerk read it carefully.

"Hurry up, hurry up!" Riggs complained. Even from here Libby heard the impatience in his voice.

But the clerk took his time. Finally he nodded. Turning, he called to someone on main deck. "Get Captain Norstad!"

Libby's heart turned over. Taking the stairs to the texas deck in one leap, she raced to her father's cabin. There she pounded on the door.

Seconds later Pa flung it open. "Libby!" Even his eyes looked concerned. "What's wrong?"

"Riggs is here!" she exclaimed as her father drew her inside his cabin. "He's got a paper—a search warrant, I think."

"Probably so." Captain Norstad's voice was calm, as if he had expected this.

"But, Pa, they're coming for you! They'll search the *Christina*."

Still her father showed no surprise. "Yes, that's what they'll do."

"They'll ask you questions." Libby's words tumbled out.

"Go and warn Caleb," Pa said.

"But the men are coming for *you*!"

A shadow passed through her father's eyes. "Libby, find Caleb. Then stay away from the men. Don't let them see your face."

Tears rose in Libby's eyes. "Pa, I'm scared. What if something happens to you?"

"Please, Libby." Captain Norstad's voice was gentle, but there was no denying his request for obedience. "After you talk to Caleb, try to get back to your room. Stay there till the men leave."

Never before had Libby disobeyed Pa's orders, but this time she waited, not wanting to leave.

"Hurry!" he said. Even now Libby heard the sounds of men coming up the stairs. Pa pushed her out the door toward the stairs on the other side of the *Christina*.

"Don't make a sound," he whispered. "Find Caleb."

Without another word Libby hurried down the steps. As she reached the deck below, she heard loud pounding on the door of her father's cabin.

"Open up!" a man called. Libby felt sure it was Riggs.

Libby ran on, searching the boiler deck for Caleb. To her relief she found him in the area where first-class passengers took their exercise.

"Riggs is here," Libby said quickly.

"I know," Caleb answered. "It's all right."

"What do you mean it's *all right*?" Libby felt angry. Caleb looked as calm as her father. Was Caleb used to this kind of thing?

"Everything will be okay," Caleb said. "Stop looking so scared."

"I'm not scared," Libby answered.

"Yes, you are. You look like a jackrabbit fleeing for your life. Go hide your face."

"Hide my face? What do you mean?"

"Go to your room," Caleb answered. "Don't let Riggs or his men see you."

"But they'll arrest Pa!"

Caleb refused to listen. Without another word he stalked off. Libby stared at his back, then took the stairs two at a time. By the time she reached the texas deck, her heart was in her throat.

Gasping for breath, Libby slipped inside her room. Quickly she pulled the shutters that hid her from the deck. Without a sound she crossed to the other side of her room and closed those shutters too.

From her father's cabin, Libby heard the sound of men's voices—angry voices making demands. Then a door opened. Crouching down next to her bed, Libby listened, every sense alert.

Rough voices and the sound of heavy feet filled the deck. As the men passed her room, Libby waited, holding her breath. Would Riggs search from one stateroom to the next? Passengers were still in bed.

Then Libby heard her father's voice. "You see?" he asked from just outside her room. "All is quiet on the river this morning."

It was a warning, Libby knew—a warning to remain where she was, making no sound.

After what seemed forever, she heard the men going down a stairway to the boiler deck just below. Libby pulled back a shutter just a crack.

Soon she opened it all the way. Standing in the doorway, she listened.

No longer could Libby hear the men. Still on bare feet, she took the few steps from the texas to the hurricane deck. As she crept forward, she heard men's voices again. Libby felt sure they were going down the wide steps at the front of the boat. Even on the thick red carpeting, their boots sounded heavy.

On her knees, Libby peered over the low railing on the hurricane deck. Though two decks away, she could hear shouted orders.

"Push it aside!" That was Riggs, standing at the bow of the boat.

When he glanced up, Libby ducked behind the railing. Soon she heard crates scraping across the deck and barrels tipped roughly over. Then someone slammed something wooden.

Rising up, Libby again looked over the railing. One of the men had thrown back the cover of a hatch near the bow. When Riggs started down into the hold, other men followed. Watching them, Libby grew more and more nervous. Captain Norstad had told Jordan to go to the engine room when the *Christina* was in port. But what about times like now? Was that what Caleb and Jordan had been doing—building a place to hide?

It bothered Libby that Riggs seemed to know where that place might be. A cold fist tightened around her heart. *When they find Jordan, they'll arrest Pa.*

Waiting for what seemed forever, Libby watched and listened. Finally she saw Riggs come up from the hold. One of his men slammed down the hatch. Crates and barrels scraped against the deck.

"Try another hatch!" That was Riggs again, and Libby felt sure he would search each section of the hold.

Following his orders, the men moved back along the side of the *Christina*. When one of them called out from near the stairway, Libby remembered. *Pa told me to stay in my room. If a man crept up the stairs, he'd find me!*

In spite of her curiosity, Libby hurried back, slipped inside her room, and pulled the shutters almost closed. Her hands trembled as she waited, listening for any sound of men coming back up the steps.

An hour later Libby sensed a change. *No more slammed hatches*, she thought. *No loud voices or men stomping up and down.* Instead, the decks seemed strangely quiet.

Tiptoeing, Libby crept out of her room to the edge of the hurricane deck. Again she knelt down and peered over the railing.

Soon Libby spied Riggs on the far end of the gangplank. When he stepped onto the landing, Libby saw only his back. Yet she knew what had happened by the way he walked. The cruel slave trader was angry. So were the men with him.

They didn't find Jordan! Libby wanted to jump up and down and dance with relief. To laugh and cry all at once. To shout the good news to the whole world. *Jordan's safe! And so is Pa! At least for the moment.*

Then Libby faced a new fear. *Riggs will come back. How? And where? And when?* Chills chased down Libby's spine just thinking about it.

A moment later another thought struck her. *If Riggs can't find where Jordan hides, how can I?*

Slowly she got to her feet and went down the stairs looking for Caleb. Once again Libby had more questions than answers.

❁

"C'mon, Libby," Caleb said after breakfast the next morning. "I'll show you how to be a runner."

"What's a runner?" Libby stood high on the hurricane deck, watching all that was going on. She wanted to explore the streets and shops of St. Louis, to meet its people, to watch the long trains of pioneer wagons leaving for the West.

"A runner drums up business for a steamboat." Caleb grinned. "We stand near the gangplank and tell people how great we are."

As he and Libby started toward the stairs, Caleb explained. In large cities steamboats competed for both passengers and freight. Captains sent boys such as Caleb onto the levees or landings to direct people to their steamboat and bring in whatever business they could.

Libby hung back. "What if Riggs is watching the *Christina*? What if he sees us out in front?"

Caleb shrugged. "He already knows we're here. Why do you think he brought that search warrant? He figures that wherever he sees me, he'll find Jordan."

"Doesn't that bother you?" Libby still hoped that Riggs wouldn't recognize her. "If Riggs knows me, too, why didn't Pa want him to see me?"

On the wide stairway leading to the main deck, Caleb grinned. "Your Pa knows that your face could get all of us arrested."

"My face?" Libby asked. "It's not *that* bad!"

"Your big brown eyes show too much. If you look scared, you'll give the rest of us away."

Still not convinced that she wanted to be a runner, Libby trailed down the stairs after Caleb.

"If Riggs comes near you, don't show him what you're thinking," Caleb went on. "You'll get Jordan in big trouble."

More than once Libby had admired Caleb for being able to hide his thoughts from slave catchers. Now Libby doubted that she could do the same. All her life she had leaped before looking and talked before thinking.

"When he searched yesterday, Riggs couldn't find Jordan." It made Libby curious. Somehow she would discover the *Christina*'s hiding place, but she knew Caleb would never tell her.

"That's why we want to stay a jump ahead of him," Caleb answered. "Riggs knows we're doing something. He knows it involves runaway slaves. If he catches us at it, he'll collect rewards for a lot of slaves. Think of all the money he'll get!"

Libby's hands tightened into fists. She felt angry toward the cruel slave trader. Angry because of the way Riggs could harm Jordan and Pa and Caleb. Angry at the fugitive slave law that gave a slave catcher the right to search for runaways even in free states.

"So how do I become a runner?" Libby asked.

"You tell people about the *Christina*." On the wide stairway leading to the main deck, Caleb stepped closer and lowered his voice. "While you're doing that, watch for Riggs."

"For *Riggs*?" Libby blurted out. Always he made her feel like a hunted animal. *If he does that to me, it must be one hundred times worse for Jordan.*

"You want me to watch for *Riggs*?" Libby asked a little too loudly.

"Shhh!" Caleb warned. "That's what I mean. You'll give us away!"

4

Unwanted Passenger

"*I* don't want to even think about Riggs!" Libby tossed her red curls and wished she could be far away from danger.

In the middle of the main deck, Caleb stopped. "You better think about him." Caleb's voice was still low. "Pretend that you're a slave trader like Riggs. If you searched a steamboat and didn't find the runaway you're looking for, what would you do next?"

Libby thought for a moment. "I'd come on board as a passenger."

"Yup!" Caleb grinned. "Riggs will probably use a different name. But all we have to do is spot him when he boards the *Christina*."

"*All!*" Libby exclaimed. "Pa says this could be the most crowded trip of the season. How many people does that mean?"

"If we do our job, there could be over three hundred, counting the crew," Caleb said.

The difficulty of finding one person among so many frightened Libby. "If we miss Riggs, he'll find out everything he wants to know. Sooner or later he'll accuse Pa of hiding a fugitive."

"That's why I need your help," Caleb told her. "If everyone was in one place at one time, it wouldn't be so hard. But there are too many places to hide. If Riggs comes on board, it's better that we know."

Caleb headed down the gangplank. "Bet I spot him before you do."

His words made finding the slave catcher a game to Libby. Though Caleb didn't want her taking part in the Underground Railroad, she'd prove that she could be useful. Maybe he'd learn to trust her.

"Tell me what to do," she said.

"I'll show you. Your pa wants a full load of freight and passengers for St. Paul. We'll get it for him."

Here, next to the water, the noise and traffic seemed overwhelming. On the levee Caleb took a place near the gangplank. "Ladies and gentlemen!" he shouted. "For the safest ride on the river, choose the *Christina*! Choose Captain Norstad, the most reliable captain on the Mississippi! Sixteen years of safe travel! Sixteen years of bringing passengers to where they want to be!"

As Libby watched, people turned their heads. Some kept walking, looking up at the steamboats as though deciding which one to take. Others stopped to listen.

"Step right up, folks!" Caleb called out. "Book your passage all the way to St. Paul!"

When passengers came close to Caleb, he talked to them. "Sign up now for the cleanest boat on the river. Food to make your mouth water! My Granny makes the pastries, and see how tall I've grown!"

As soon as Caleb answered their questions, he guided the first-class passengers toward the gangplank and told them to find the office. He brought the deckers, or deck passengers, over to a young man.

"Here you are, folks! Mr. Martin will help you."

Called the mud clerk because in most towns he stood in the mud, young Martin checked freight on and off the *Christina*. He also took the fares of deck passengers.

As a horse-drawn wagon filled with crates rumbled past, Caleb changed his cry. "Ship your freight all the way to Minnesota Territory! We'll get your valuable goods wherever you want in the fastest time!"

"Whoa!" The teamster pulled back on the reins. "Whoa!" Coming to a stop, he gazed up at the *Christina*. "To St. Paul, eh?" he asked Caleb.

"Yup! Safe handling for all your freight! No sitting on a wharf waiting for another boat. Straight from St. Louis to St. Paul!"

"How much?"

Turning, Caleb motioned to the mud clerk, and Martin stepped forward. Soon he and the man reached an agreement. Deckhands from the *Christina* began loading the crates.

Before long, a passenger led a cow up the gangplank. Tossing her head against the rope around her neck, the cow rolled her eyes in fear. On his back another man carried a slatted crate with chickens.

Watching Caleb's success, Libby gathered up her courage. "Take the *Christina* to St. Paul!" she shouted. "Safest boat on the river!"

The moment the words left her lips, Libby wished she could call them back. At times she found it hard to believe that any steamboat could be safe. Yet if there was such a thing, she felt sure it would be her father's.

Once again Libby called out. This time she thought about Auntie Vi. During four long years, she had tried to turn Libby into a proper young lady. *What would Auntie say if she saw me now?*

In the middle of a sentence, Libby choked. The passengers listening to her turned away.

Moments later Libby's father walked out on the main deck. When he saw Libby on the levee, he waved at her. As Libby's shyness fell away, she knew what to say.

"Ladies and gentlemen!" she called out. "Best father—best steamboat captain in the business! Ride the *Christina*, and know your captain cares about you!"

Turning toward the steamboat, Libby saw Pa's face. When he dropped one eyelid in a long slow wink, Libby winked back. Seeing his grin, she felt warm with his love.

The next deckers who came along stopped to talk with her. When they bought tickets from Martin, Libby felt excited. She actually could do this!

As she kept on calling, Libby watched every passenger who approached the *Christina*. She paid little attention to the women and the tall, heavyset men. During the next hour, she saw at least three short, slender men, but none of them reminded her of Riggs.

Throughout the morning, workers hurried up and down the gangplank loading freight. The crates and barrels going all the way to St. Paul went into the hull. Deckhands opened hatches and slid the freight down ramps into the hold.

While Caleb kept watch, Libby took a break for lunch. As she passed an open hatch on the main deck, she looked down into the hole. Because the *Christina* needed to go into the shallow waters of the upper Mississippi, the hull was only five feet deep. It was divided into compartments by long, solid pieces of wood called bulkheads. These bulkheads stretched from the bow of the boat to the stern and provided the framework for the hull. Bulkheads also helped the crew load the boat in such a way that the freight didn't shift around.

When Libby finished eating, Samson followed her down the gangplank. "Stay!" she told him when she reached the levee. In spite of his gentle nature, Samson was so large that he might frighten away passengers. Samson tipped his head and dropped down next to Libby.

"I'll watch for Riggs while you eat," Libby whispered to Caleb. With a bound he was up the gangplank and out of sight.

The midday sun was warm now. Standing on the levee, Libby looked around. As far as she could see in either direction, steamboats lay with their bows nosed into the levee. When Libby compared the activity around the *Christina*, she felt good. She and Caleb had brought in more than enough business for her father.

In the next instant, her warm feelings vanished. Directly ahead of her, a well-dressed man walked straight toward the *Christina*. With every sure-of-himself step he took, Libby felt more uneasy. Short and slender, the man carried a cane, but he didn't need it for walking.

That's Riggs! Libby thought.

Then Libby saw that the man had a handlebar mustache. The mustache spread wide and curled up on both sides. *That can't be Riggs,* Libby thought. *He couldn't possibly grow such a big mustache since yesterday!*

Moments later Libby changed her mind again. *He could wear a false mustache!*

Libby whirled around. *Caleb, where are you?*

Not catching even a glimpse of him, Libby turned back. Near the gangplank at least twenty or thirty passengers waited to board. The man who looked like Riggs stopped behind them.

If he comes on board, he'll hunt for Jordan! Libby thought frantically.

Again she turned toward the *Christina. If only I could race up the gangplank, search for Caleb, call his name!*

Filled with panic, Libby stared at the passengers again. The crowd had grown even larger. While deckers waited to pay their fare, first-class passengers moved around them and up the gangplank.

Just then a deckhand carrying a large trunk stepped in front of Libby. A second man followed with another trunk on his shoulder. Desperately, Libby moved from side to side, trying to see around them.

The moment the deckhands walked on, Libby searched the crowd again. Nowhere did she spy the man she thought was Riggs. *He has to be here!*

Just then Libby saw a nail keg near the gangplank. Racing over, she jumped onto it. With the added height, she had a better view of the entire crowd.

As she studied each face, Libby felt sick. *The man who looks like Riggs is gone!*

The minute Caleb returned, Libby told him what had happened.

"You don't know whether the man boarded or not?" Caleb asked.

Libby still felt upset. "He stopped toward the back of the crowd. He could have taken another steamboat. Or he might have gone up the gangplank when I couldn't see."

"What did he look like?" Caleb asked.

"Exactly like Riggs, except for one thing. He had a handlebar mustache with a stiff curl on each side. Maybe it's a disguise."

Caleb nodded. "Good thinking. A big mustache would hide the frown lines in his face."

"So what do we do?" Libby asked as a man with a gray-and-white beard set down his bags in front of young Martin.

Heavyset and of medium height, the man wore a rumpled brown suit and a beaver hat. His small, round glasses had settled halfway down his nose.

"First-class passengers register in the office," Martin told him.

Bending down, the man picked up a black leather bag and a carpetbag—a cloth suitcase with handles. As he started up the gangplank, Martin called after him. "Are you a doctor, by any chance?"

When the man nodded, Martin spoke again. "The captain will be glad to know we have a medical man on board. If there's an emergency, can we call on you?"

"Certainly, certainly. My name's Fenton. I'd be glad to help." With a tip of his hat, the doctor passed up the gangplank.

In that moment Libby felt a hand drop on her shoulder.

5

Scary Thoughts

"It looks like you two have done a good job," Captain Norstad said.

"Thank you, sir," Caleb answered respectfully.

Just then Libby noticed a man and a woman wearing the warm, heavy clothing of immigrants heading toward the *Christina*. A girl about Libby's age trailed behind.

Not far from the steamboat, the man stopped to stare at the letters on the large wooden box surrounding the paddle wheel. "Yah. The *Christina*. That is what the man said."

In front of young Martin, the immigrant set down his trunk. "Good day," he told the clerk. "You go to Minnesota Territory?"

"We leave at four o'clock," Martin answered.

Digging deep beneath layers of clothing, the man pulled out a money holder. "Franz Meyer," he said as the clerk started to write. Mr. Meyer nodded toward his wife, then the girl with white-blond hair. "Frau Meyer. Our daughter Elsa."

Before Mr. Meyer could pay his fare, Libby's father stepped over to him. "I'm the captain," he said. "I'm sorry, but we are full."

"Please, Herr Captain," Mr. Meyer answered. "Someone told me that you are an honorable man. That the *Christina* is good for—" He waved a hand toward his wife and daughter.

"We try to be good for families," Captain Norstad answered.

"He said that if I took my family with you, we would be safe from the—" Mr. Meyer paused. As though struggling for the word, he held up his money holder.

Captain Norstad understood. "From the pickpockets and thieves who want to steal everything you have. If we know who they are, we keep them off the *Christina*."

"Yah." Mr. Meyer looked pleased that the captain understood. "We need to go to Minnesota Territory. To Red Wing we need to go."

"I'm sorry," Captain Norstad answered. "Every room is taken."

"We want to be on deck," Mr. Meyer answered. "In any small place we stay. Please, Herr Captain, I need to find good land before it is all gone."

Captain Norstad sighed. "I want to help you, but we are already crowded."

Suddenly Mrs. Meyer stepped forward. "Please, Herr Captain. We are not much room. Me." She pointed to herself, then to the girl Libby's age. "Elsa."

Elsa looked thin enough to vanish at any moment. Beneath her blue eyes were light gray shadows, as if charcoal had smudged her pale skin. As Libby stared at the girl, their gaze met. When Elsa smiled, her face lit up.

"I don't want to load the boat so it isn't safe," Captain Norstad said.

"We have not much luggage." Mr. Meyer looked toward the trunk on the ground. His wife held out a large cloth suitcase with handles, and Elsa showed a smaller carpetbag.

Oh, take them, Pa! Libby wanted to say. Just looking at Elsa, she felt sure they could be friends. But Libby knew better than to interfere with her father's business.

For a moment Captain Norstad thought about it. Finally he

nodded. "Welcome aboard, Herr Meyer. Frau Meyer. Elsa. We trust you will have a good trip with us."

A grateful smile crossed Mr. Meyer's face. As if to add his welcome, Samson edged forward. Palm up, Elsa held out her hand, and Samson sniffed it.

Afraid that he would jump up, Libby laid her hand on his neck and twisted her fingers in his long hair.

"He is your hound?" Elsa asked.

"My dog," Libby answered. "His name is Samson."

"Samson," Elsa repeated, her accent strong. "Good dog."

As Samson edged closer, Elsa petted his head. Samson's great open mouth seemed to grin his approval.

Elsa laughed. "You want to be friends, yah?"

Samson's soft woof seemed like a yes, and Elsa laughed again.

"I want to work for our passage," Mr. Meyer told Captain Norstad.

Libby's father nodded, and the clerk entered the names of the family on his list. When money changed hands, Libby knew it was less than the usual fare because Mr. Meyer would help with carrying wood whenever the steamboat took on fuel.

"*Danke,*" he said at last. His "thank you" sounded like *dunk-uh*. After shaking the captain's hand, Mr. Meyer once more balanced his trunk on his shoulder.

As the Meyer family walked up the gangplank, Samson started after them. When Libby called to him, Samson stopped. Yet he followed them with his eyes until they disappeared around the cargo on deck.

"No more passengers," the captain told the mud clerk. "Not another person. Not one more piece of freight."

"There are still a few open spaces on deck, sir," Martin answered. "Most captains take on everyone they can get."

"And the immigrant families are so crowded that they lose their children overboard."

"Not if their parents watch them, sir. If they—"

The captain's look stopped him midsentence. "I've given my orders," he said to the clerk. "Do you question them?"

"Yes, sir," Martin said quickly. "I mean, no, sir."

"Then we understand each other." When Captain Norstad started up the gangplank, even Libby stepped out of his way.

As though trying to make amends, the young clerk bowed toward Libby. Caleb stepped between them.

"I need to check the passenger list." Reaching out, Caleb took the list as if there could be no doubt about his authority to see it. Quickly he turned the pages, scanning the long list of deck passengers.

If Riggs had come on board, Caleb gave no hint that he knew. Finally he returned the list. As he and Libby walked up the gangplank, Caleb spoke low in her ear. "I'll take a look at the first-class passenger list too."

"Then I'll find Elsa." Libby was eager to make friends.

The main deck was crowded with freight and the stacks of wood that fueled the steamboat. Deckhands had kept open a path for first-class passengers to reach the stairway to the deck above. Except for that path, there were only narrow spaces for moving around. As Libby searched out walkways, Samson followed close behind.

Suddenly one of the deckhands bumped into Libby. "Watch where you're going!" he said roughly, then stopped. "Sorry, Miss," he mumbled quickly, as if realizing she was the captain's daughter.

Just then Samson passed Libby and squeezed through narrow places she barely saw. Following the dog, she watched for Elsa and her family.

Deck passengers had chosen their own living areas, settling down wherever they could find a few feet between barrels and crates. On most steamboats, deckers slept wherever they could. Wanting to provide a better place for them, Captain Norstad had taken the unusual step of building bunks in a small room on the main deck.

When Libby checked there, she found that all of the bunks had been taken by the first deckers onto the *Christina*. Before long, Samson brought Libby to the Meyer family. Along one side, near the engine room and close to the edge of the deck, Mr. Meyer had made a place for his family.

Mrs. Meyer sat on top of the trunk with the frightened cow owned by another passenger directly behind her. As Libby watched, the cow swished her tail in Mrs. Meyer's face.

Mr. Meyer had climbed onto a nearby pile of wood. Careful not to bump his head, he lay in the narrow space between the top of the wood and the underside of the deck above. As soon as the paddle wheels started, he would feel the vibration in every bone of his body.

Even worse, the family was close to the noise and danger of the steam engines and boilers. If the boilers exploded, it was usually the deckers who received terrible injuries or died.

But it was Elsa who worried Libby most. Sitting on the carpetbags, she was only a few feet from the edge of the deck and a foot or two above the river. No railing protected her.

Seeing Elsa, Libby gulped. It was exactly what Pa didn't want. It would take only one jolt of the steamboat, and Elsa would tumble into the cold water, never to be seen again.

What if the Christina *strikes a sand bar or hits a stump?* Libby didn't want to think about it. Yet there was something she knew. *If Pa hadn't let them on, they would have found an even more crowded boat.*

Libby tried to push aside her scared feelings. "Please," she said to Elsa. "When we start, come away from the edge."

"The edge?" Clearly the other girl did not know what that meant.

"The water," Libby said. She pointed down. "You fall in."

This time Elsa understood. Picking up the carpetbags, she pointed to a narrow place on the trunk next to her mother.

"There it is safe?" she asked.

Libby nodded.

"Then you sit there," Elsa said. "And I sit on the trunk when you go."

As Libby squeezed onto the trunk, Elsa again sat down next to the water.

"Where are you from?" Libby asked, though she thought she knew.

Elsa smiled shyly, as if wanting Libby to become a friend. "My family and I, we come from Germany."

"You speak English well," Libby said.

Elsa nodded. "Before we come, we practice. Every day we have lessons on ship."

As the girls talked together, Mrs. Meyer stood up. When she motioned to her, Libby also stood up.

Opening the trunk, Mrs. Meyer took out a plate, then a jar of herring. Like other families who were deckers, the Meyers had brought along their own food. Watching them, Libby wondered how they would make their food last long enough for the journey.

Using the trunk as a table, Mrs. Meyer forked four small pieces of herring onto the plate. When she and Libby took their places on the trunk again, Mr. Meyer slid down from the woodpile and stood next to Libby.

"We celebrate," he said. "We are on the boat to Minnesota Territory. God has brought us this far."

When he bowed his head to pray, the others did also. After blessing the food, Mr. Meyer offered the plate to Libby. "You like herring too?"

"Yes, I do," Libby said. Then she drew back. *I can't take what little food they have.*

"Thank you," she answered quickly. "You are very kind, but I just ate my dinner." Instead of taking a piece, she passed the plate to Mrs. Meyer.

As if enjoying every bite, each member of the family ate slowly. When they finished, the one small piece of herring that Libby did not eat remained on the plate. Carefully Mrs. Meyer forked it back into the jar.

❋

Not long after, Caleb joined them. He grinned at Elsa, then spoke to Libby. "Your pa wants us to do our lesson before we leave St. Louis. He said we should visit the courtroom where Dred Scott made his first appeal for freedom."

"What did you find out about Riggs?" Libby asked as she and Caleb left the *Christina*.

"There isn't a Riggs on either the first-class or decker list," Caleb told her. "But I'm not surprised. It doesn't seem likely that he would use his own name."

A scared feeling tightened Libby's throat. "What should we try next?"

"We have to search until we find him. Or at least till we're sure he's *not* with us."

Again Libby thought about the three hundred people on board. "That's like looking for a needle in a haystack."

"I know," Caleb answered. "But we can try. The best place to look is in the main cabin at mealtimes."

Libby agreed, but she was the only one who could do it. Both Jordan and Caleb ate elsewhere. Yet there was a problem, even for her. There were two serving times for every meal. "If Riggs eats at a different time, I won't see him."

"That might be exactly what he does," Caleb answered as they crossed the cobblestone levee. "Or Riggs might change times, just to throw us off. He has to know we'll be looking for him."

A short distance beyond a row of proud new buildings lay the St. Louis County Courthouse. As Libby and Caleb drew close to the steps, she looked around.

Today no one had gathered to auction slaves, but Libby remembered their last visit. Here she and Caleb had seen Jordan the first time. Tall and proud, he had stood at the top of the steps. In that terrible moment of being sold as a slave, Jordan had reminded Libby of royalty.

"Where is he?" she asked, and Caleb knew who she meant.

"Still hiding," he answered. "Jordan won't show his face till we're far from here."

"Did he want to come with us?"

"He said, 'Caleb, you look inside that courthouse real good.

I wants to see it through your eyes.' "

"Where's he hiding?" Libby asked.

Caleb brushed her question aside. "You know I can't tell you."

But Libby couldn't shake off her wondering about Jordan. "Is there some way you could get a message to his mother?" she asked. "Could you possibly tell her that Jordan is free and planning to come after her?"

"It would be awfully dangerous," Caleb answered. "But there are a lot of free blacks who help runaways. Maybe Jordan knows of someone who can get a message through."

As Caleb pulled open the large door of the courthouse, he seemed deep in thought. Since the age of nine, Caleb had worked on the Underground Railroad. Now Libby wondered, *How many fugitives has he helped?*

In a long hallway, Caleb asked directions to the place where the first two Dred Scott trials were held. He and Libby learned that the large courtroom had taken up the entire west wing. Because the ceiling needed more support, that part of the building had been divided into a corridor and two smaller courtrooms.

"Dred Scott is a small man," Caleb told Libby. "Less than five feet tall, from what people say. But he's taken on a big fight."

In one of the smaller courtrooms, Libby tried to imagine what it had been like for Dred Scott. For almost nine years, he had lived in a free state and a free territory. *How did it feel to be a slave and stand before the high, long desk where the judge sat? What was Dred Scott thinking about as he asked for the freedom he so strongly believed should be his?*

As Libby and Caleb went back outside, Caleb was silent, as though not wanting to talk. It surprised Libby, for usually Caleb took little time to think things through. Then he acted quickly.

When at last he spoke, Caleb spit out his words. "A person like Dred Scott—a person like Jordan to be called *property*! How could the Supreme Court of the United States make such a decision?"

Sparks of anger lit Caleb's eyes. "If the federal Supreme Court had made a different decision, they could have changed history. They could have said, 'Our country believes in freedom for *everyone*!' Instead, their decision is driving slavery and antislavery people farther apart!"

Caleb isn't afraid to think things through, Libby decided. Her discovery came as a surprise, and she liked him better for it. More than once, Libby had called Caleb the strangest boy she knew because he was unlike anyone else she had met. Then his grandmother told her, "To understand Caleb, you have to understand what he believes in."

Now his beliefs made Libby uneasy. *Where will his thinking lead Caleb? What might it cause him to do?*

When they returned to the *Christina,* Caleb left Libby without a word. Later she searched for him because there was something that still bothered her. She found him nailing the cover on a large box. "Caleb?" she asked. "I need to talk to you."

When he drove the last nail into the box, Caleb dropped down on a keg. Libby found a nearby crate. Her scared feelings tightened her throat as she asked, "What would be worse than Pa going to jail?"

6

The Secret Hideaway

*C*aleb stared at her. "Don't you know, Libby? Don't you have any idea?"

Libby shook her head. "No, Caleb," she said softly. "I don't know."

"Then I'll tell you. It would be far worse if your Pa gave in."

"Gave in?" Libby asked, not sure what Caleb was talking about.

"Your pa stands for something," Caleb said. "He stands for good things—the right things. If he gave in on what he believes, a lot of other people might do the same thing."

"What do you mean?" Libby asked.

"Your pa believes that every person should be free."

Libby nodded. She knew that.

"But he doesn't believe it just with his head," Caleb went on. "He believes it with his heart. Your pa believes in helping runaway slaves, even though it costs him something."

"Costs him *something*!" Libby exclaimed. "It could cost him a lot!"

"Yup!" Caleb agreed with her. "It could cost him everything."

"*Everything?*" Libby whispered. Her tongue frozen by fear, she stumbled over the words. "Do I understand what you're saying?"

"Maybe." Caleb's blue eyes met hers, and he did not look away.

"Are you saying that Pa could give his life for what he believes?"

"Some people have."

"Elijah Lovejoy," Libby answered. "That newspaper editor from Alton, Illinois."

Caleb nodded. Elijah Lovejoy was Caleb's hero, a newspaperman who stood up for what he believed.

To Libby there could not possibly be anything worse than having something happen to Pa. *He's my whole life!*

As tears welled up in Libby's eyes, she turned away, not wanting Caleb to see. Instead, he surprised her. "Libby," he said softly, "I love your father too."

Libby turned back. Tears blurred her vision, and she could not speak.

"When my parents died, I lived with Gran," Caleb explained. "She needed to earn money to support both of us. Your pa gave Gran a job as head pastry cook on the *Christina*. He even gave me a chance to earn money as a cabin boy."

Caleb leaned forward as though wanting to make sure Libby understood. "Your pa is kind, Libby. He's the kindest man I know. That's why he cares so much about what happens to slaves."

Already Libby had learned about the unusual arrangement between Caleb and her father. Because they believed the same way about slavery, Pa trusted Caleb to help runaways. Without talking about every fugitive that came to the *Christina*, Pa agreed with what Caleb did to protect them. That in turn protected Pa when slave catchers tried to question him.

Libby swallowed hard against the fresh torrent of tears that would destroy her. Again she turned away.

"Look at me, Libby." Caleb sounded much older than his thirteen years. He waited until she met his gaze. "Your pa does his best to be careful. He doesn't take any foolish chances. But you're forgetting something. It's God who takes care of him."

God? Libby thought. *How can God be enough protection for Pa?*

"Your Pa is like a father to me, Libby." Caleb's voice was soft now. "Like a real Pa. If something hurts him, it would hurt me too."

Libby swallowed hard against the lump in her throat. "Thanks, Caleb," she said, choking on the words.

As she headed for the stairs, great sobs tore at Libby's throat. By the time she reached the texas deck, she could barely see the way. Inside her room Libby threw herself facedown on the bed.

No! Nothing will happen to Pa! Sobs ripped through Libby's body. *He'll stand up for what he believes, but nothing will happen to him!*

By the time Libby stopped crying, dusk had settled around the *Christina.* The beautiful white steamboat had put out from St. Louis without her even noticing.

Libby stumbled to her feet and splashed water over her face. Her skin was blotchy and her eyes swollen, but she was glad that Caleb had explained.

At the sound of scratching, Libby looked through the window. Samson stood on the other side, and Libby opened the door. Dropping to her knees, she threw her arms around his neck.

When Pa had given her the Newfoundland, she hadn't wanted the monstrous dog. Now he seemed like the best friend in the whole world. As though understanding that Libby felt upset, Samson stretched out his long tongue and tried to lick her face. Libby edged back. "Oh, ick!"

Samson's wide grin stretched from ear to ear. In spite of the comfort he gave, Libby's thoughts leapfrogged ahead. *Where does Jordan hide?* she wondered for the one hundredth time. *If I could find his secret place, I'd know where any fugitive might be.*

❄

In the middle of the night, Libby woke up feeling cold right into her bones. Shivering, she pulled her quilts over her head, curled up into a ball, and tried to go back to sleep.

Yet sleep would not come to her. Even here, high on the texas deck, she felt a slight vibration from the paddle wheels. What was it like for Mr. Meyer, sleeping on the woodpile and feeling the vibration in every bone?

And Mrs. Meyer. If she leaned back in her sleep, she would only fall into the cow. But what about Elsa? Had she stayed away from the edge of the deck?

Her new friend looked too pale, and thin besides. Libby dreaded the cold the family would find as they steamed north. Even here, a short distance above St. Louis, the damp night air crept through the windows. With no heat in her room, Libby had nothing but quilts to stop her shivers. *Does Elsa have even that?*

Libby tried to remember the size of the family's trunk. It carried food, as well as tools for a new life. How many quilts could it hold? Not many, Libby knew, if any at all.

They'll gather around the stove in their deck room, Libby told herself. In that way, too, her father had been unusual, wanting to make a place for deckers to warm themselves. Yet those who claimed first right would not give up their space.

I could bring Elsa a quilt. As quickly as the idea came, Libby pushed it aside. *The farther north we go, the colder I'll be. I'll need every quilt I have.*

As Libby turned over, the dry corn shucks in her mattress rustled. The ropes stretched across the bed frame kept her mattress comfortable. Every morning Libby tightened those ropes when she made her bed.

Sleep tight. Don't let the bedbugs bite! Libby almost giggled. *And if they do, hit 'em with a shoe!*

Snuggling down, she felt grateful for the way Pa cared for her. Then a question came. *Does that mean Elsa's father doesn't care for her?*

Again Libby pushed away the thought. Mr. Meyer was doing everything he could. Like other immigrants, he and his family wanted to leave their old life behind. They had given up all they had for their dream of a better life in America.

Ashamed of herself now, Libby swung her feet out of bed. When she touched the cold floor, her toes tingled. Quickly she dressed, then fumbled in the dark to pull her warmest quilt off the bed.

Quietly she opened her door. Samson lay on the deck outside. As Libby started down the stairs, he followed.

When she reached the main deck, Libby found it even more crowded than during the day. By the light of the moon, she saw people huddled wherever they could find a space.

Deep shadows made it hard to know where all of them were. As Libby struggled to find her way, she stepped on someone.

"Ouch!" he muttered. "Watch where you're going!"

"Sorry!" Libby said, and kept on. But when she stepped on someone else, she knew it was no use. Bending down, she spoke into Samson's ear. "Find Elsa."

Between barrels, crates, and sleeping bodies Samson picked his way. Wherever he stepped, Libby followed. When they came to the long, sheet-iron stove provided for the deckers, Libby saw it was just as she feared. Everyone who could get around the stove was there, but Elsa was not among them.

Samson led Libby on, and at last they came to the Meyer family. Mr. Meyer lay on top of the bumpy woodpile. Mrs. Meyer sat on the trunk with her back against the cow, and Elsa was squeezed in beside her. With her mother's arm around her, Elsa hugged herself as if to find warmth. Her eyes were wide open as she trembled with cold.

Quickly Libby placed the quilt around her. As Libby tucked it in, Elsa moved the quilt so that it also covered her mother.

"Danke, Libby." Elsa's teeth chattered. "I cannot say enough thanks."

As Libby turned to leave, she remembered how close the family was to the engine room. *Maybe it'd be easier going through there*, she thought. *At least there'd be a space to walk*. She could go in the door on the deck side and out through the cargo area.

Lying directly in front of a paddle wheel, the engine room vibrated with its own noise and the slap of the great paddle wheels. Here and there a lantern hung, giving men light to work.

Libby and Samson slipped past them, moving without sound. One man raised his hand, waving to Libby. The others kept on working.

Soon Libby passed through the second door into the cargo room. Near the machinery at the edge of that area, Libby noticed an open hatch. The wooden door swung up, creating a hole in the floor.

Strange, Libby thought. *I've never seen that hatch before.* Stepping back, she looked at it. *How is it usually hidden?*

Nearby was a small but heavy-looking piece of machinery. As though to give it more strength, the machine was mounted on a piece of wood. Curious now, Libby took a lantern from the engine room and brought it close.

Setting the lantern on the floor, she knelt down. With both hands she pushed at the wood base under the machinery. Suddenly it moved!

Hardly daring to hope, Libby tested it out. Sure enough, the machine moved with little effort on her part.

With growing excitement, Libby held up the lantern again. If the hatch was closed, the machine could be swung into place over the hatch!

I've got it! Libby thought. She wanted to sing, to dance, to shout. *I've found Jordan's hiding place!* Now Caleb would have to let her take part in the Underground Railroad.

Filled with glee, Libby held the lantern over the hole. A ladder led downward and disappeared into the darkness. The space below lay between the outside of the hull and a bulkhead, the long wooden piece that ran the length of the *Christina*. Libby knew that each section between bulkheads needed its own hatch.

Somehow someone had made a secret room, or possibly more than one room! Whatever had been done, Riggs and those who searched must have missed this hidden space in the hull.

For the first time, Libby wondered why the hatch had been left open. To give a way of escape? To protect fugitives from being trapped? If the *Christina* crashed into something, the hold would fill immediately with water.

Libby knew that Caleb trusted Osborne, the chief engineer. Did Osborne hire only men who would not talk about the secret hideaway?

With the lantern still in her hand, Libby stretched out her foot and placed it on a rung of the ladder. Then she realized she couldn't climb a ladder without using both hands.

Setting the lantern as close to the hole as she dared, Libby started down. Above her Samson woofed softly, as though warning her not to go. Peering into the hole, he stood like a guard, watching over her.

About five feet down, Libby stepped onto the floor of the hull. The space was narrow, perhaps only three or four feet wide. Samson stretched out his paw, setting it on the first rung of the ladder.

"Stay," Libby said, afraid that he would hurt himself if he jumped into the small space. Samson stepped back, but whimpered, wanting to follow.

"Stay," Libby commanded again. Samson flopped down on his stomach, giving Libby more light. Barely able to see, she looked around.

On one side Libby felt the deep, wood beams of the hull. On the other side was the strong, wooden bulkhead that stretched from bow to stern. Neither of these could possibly have an opening.

On the remaining two sides, Libby felt solid wood. *There has to be a door!* she thought. *Or maybe two doors, one on each side. Doors that open into a hiding place!*

Standing next to the ladder, Libby looked up. Only a faint glow from the lantern shone down the hole. Using the tiny bit of light, Libby turned to the solid wall on her left.

Stretching as high as she could reach, Libby moved her hands across the wood. Finding nothing, she moved her hands down, again going from one side to the other. Whenever her fingers found an uneven spot, she pressed the wood and felt all around it, hoping for a hidden latch.

She had almost reached the bottom of the wall when Samson

whined. Looking up, Libby saw him on his feet, as though warning her. Moments later Libby heard footsteps. Quickly she backed away from the ladder. As she crouched in the deepest shadow, she heard a voice.

"Looking for mice?" a man asked Samson.

Mice? Libby thought.

Again Samson whined, as though pleading with Libby to come up. In the next instant, she heard the thud of the hatch dropping down. As darkness closed in around her, a scream rose in Libby's throat.

7

Hidden Monsters

*J*ust as quickly, Libby swallowed her scream. *I can't make noise!* she told herself over and over.

I'm not supposed to be down here! What if there's danger? What if someone closed the hatch because the Christina *is being searched?*

Whatever she did, Libby could not give the hiding place away. Yet terror welled up within her. A terror unlike anything she had ever known.

Trying to calm herself, Libby drew a deep breath, but her panic did not go away. Instead, she started shaking.

I want to have courage, Libby thought. *But how do I get courage in a place like this?*

As though to protect herself, Libby covered her face with her hands. When she felt her fingers tremble against her eyes, she knew how frightened she was.

In the next moment, Libby found herself praying as she had seldom prayed before. *Can God see me down in this dark hole? Does He know how scared I am?*

If only Samson were with me. He'd try to lick my face and make me laugh.

Then Libby knew that all her wishes wouldn't do a bit of good. Like it or not, she had to find a way to escape.

Feeling around in the darkness, Libby found the ladder. Taking hold with both hands, she started climbing. Soon she bumped her head on the hatch.

Balancing herself on the ladder, Libby reached up. Using both hands, she pushed with all her strength. The hatch would not move.

Libby pounded against the wood. *Maybe it's just stuck!*

But all her pounding did no good. Before long, Libby's knuckles felt sore, and she had to stop.

"Samson!" she called, forgetting that she might be heard by the wrong person. If Samson were there, he gave no answering bark.

Then Libby remembered. *It's the middle of the night! No one will know that I've disappeared!*

Slowly Libby climbed back down the ladder. Using the rungs as a guide to give direction, she knelt down on the hull. Facing the wall on the left side of the ladder, she ran her hands across the bottom third. Again she pressed any small bump in the wood, searching for a secret opening.

When at last she found it, Libby almost didn't recognize it. Next to the floor, the opening was so small that she nearly missed it. *Is it a mouse hole?* Libby wondered. It had that shape. She dreaded poking her finger inside. *Maybe a mouse will bite me!*

Then Libby knew she had no choice. Expecting sharp teeth to chomp down on her finger, she pushed it into the hole. On the other side of the wall, she felt a small but strong piece of wood.

With growing excitement Libby stretched her finger as far as she could reach in either direction. *A latch! It has to be a latch!*

Pushing at the wood every which way, she finally discovered the secret. As she prodded the underside of the latch, it lifted. In that instant the wall moved. When Libby pushed against the wood, it moved again.

It's a door! Libby thought, as the wood swung inward. Greatly relieved, she crawled through the opening.

Feeling around, Libby tried to discover where she was. On her left were the wide, strong beams of the inside of the hull. On her right, she again felt the long, upright piece of wood that was the bulkhead. Whatever the room was, it ran along the side of the boat.

Libby tried standing up. Taller than most girls her age, she bumped her head. When she knelt down, she found that someone had laid out planks to make a smooth floor.

Libby started to crawl. Before long, the walls of the long, narrow space seemed to close in around her. Feeling desperate, she wondered if she'd ever find a way to escape. *What if I'm locked down here forever?*

Then something scampered nearby. Libby yelped. *A mouse? What is it?*

Suddenly she had no doubt that a mouse was down there with her. Hadn't the man even said there might be mice?

"Mice," he said. More than one. That's even worse.

Panic washed over Libby. *Maybe they're looking at me right now. When I stretch out my hand, they'll run right over it!*

Libby's knees turned to jelly. Again she started to shake. Then, as if paralyzed, she could not move. All she could think about were the mice. "Oh, God, help me!" she cried out.

In the darkness her voice seemed to fall away. Yet in that moment, something changed. From some place long ago—a memory Libby couldn't quite recall—she seemed to hear words.

"Fear thou not."

Do not fear? Libby's heart raced with fear.

"I am with thee."

"You are with me?" Libby asked. "Here in this dark hole? Here, where no one knows that I am?"

"Be not dismayed; for I am thy God."

"God, is it really you?" Only then did Libby realize she had spoken aloud. "And you truly will help me?"

From somewhere deep in her memory, the answer came. *"I will strengthen thee, yea, I will help thee."*

Libby clung to the words. As she said them to herself, she felt stronger.

Once more something scurried in the darkness. Something very close. Again Libby's heart pounded. Yet instead of crying out, she kept repeating the words. Crawling on, she tried to think about God instead of her fears.

At last Libby saw a dim light ahead of her. Soon she reached another opening like the one where she had climbed down. As Libby started up the ladder, a lantern swung down toward her face.

"Libby!" Caleb's voice was a whisper. "What on earth are you doing here?"

Libby's giggle was part nervousness. She was awfully relieved to see him.

"You're all right?" Caleb asked as she climbed out of the hole.

Libby looked around. She had come up outside the baggage room behind the wide stairway to the boiler deck. Only Caleb and Samson were there.

"I'm all right now," Libby answered.

But Caleb looked scared. "When Samson came to me, he led me to the other hatch—the one next to the engine room." Caleb broke off, as if remembering that Libby wasn't supposed to know about this place.

"Someone closed the hatch," Libby said. "Did he swing the machinery back over the opening?"

When Caleb nodded, Libby knew that something had changed between them. "Samson whimpered and scratched away at the base of the machine. I opened the hatch, but you weren't there."

Again a scared look filled Caleb's eyes. He was so good about hiding his feelings from slave catchers that it surprised Libby. Inside, she felt a warm glow. *Caleb cares*, she thought. *He really cares about what happens to me. Maybe he even likes me.* But she didn't dare hope.

"I didn't know what happened," Caleb went on. "You could have fallen over the side of the boat."

After seeing Elsa on the main deck, Libby knew how easy it was to jump to that idea. "But I didn't," she said. "When I got locked in, I tried to find a way out."

"Libby, whatever possessed you?" Caleb whispered, but he was still upset. "What possessed you to go down into the hold in the middle of the night?"

Now that Libby thought about it, she realized that she had been foolish. Then she remembered her reason for going down. "I wanted to find where Jordan hid," she said. "I wanted to know where you put fugitives if someone like Riggs comes to visit."

"And you found a mouse."

Libby nodded.

As Caleb studied her face, she realized how she must look. Dirty. Her dress torn. Her cheeks streaked from crying.

"Are you okay, Libby?" he asked.

Surprised at the caring in his voice, Libby nodded, unable to speak. She remembered how she had planned to hold her knowledge of this place over Caleb. Now there was no pride in her, no wanting to say, "I got the better of you, Caleb Whitney."

Instead, Libby remembered the words she had seemed to hear in the darkness. *Maybe there's more to knowing God than I thought.*

She wanted to ask Caleb about it. He believed in God. He could tell her. But Libby was afraid to admit how little she knew.

⚜

Early the next morning, Libby learned that cold air had moved down from the north. Even now, on a sunny day, the air felt the touch of winter instead of spring. Yet with the windows and door closed, the sun warmed Captain Norstad's cabin.

When Libby looked around, she felt proud of her place on the *Christina. I was born to be the captain's daughter*, she thought. *If Ma were here, she would be called the First Lady*. Remembering Elsa's crowded spot, Libby felt glad that she was not living on the deck of the steamboat.

As soon as Caleb came for the day's lessons, Pa took out a

newspaper. By the way he unfolded it, Libby knew he was still upset about the Dred Scott decision.

"I want to be sure that both of you understand what the Supreme Court decision means," he said. "Chief Justice Taney ruled that as a slave, Dred Scott is not a citizen of the United States. That means he has no right to bring a suit on any matter to a federal court."

"It denies one group of people our basic American rights!" Caleb was also upset.

"That's true," Captain Norstad answered. "According to the decision, Dred Scott has never been free because slaves are personal property. The decision also says that Congress has no right to ban the spread of slavery in new territories."

Captain Norstad put down the newspaper. "To understand how serious this decision is, we need to think about our founding fathers. What did they want when they asked for their own freedom? Libby, you remember the words, don't you?"

In her Chicago school, Libby had memorized part of the Declaration of Independence. A few weeks before, she and Pa and Caleb had talked about the words: " 'We hold these truths to be self-evident, that all men are created equal—' "

"Equal!" Caleb interrupted. "The Dred Scott decision says that slaves have no constitutional rights! It's the same as saying that some of us are better than others. That's not true!"

Again Libby remembered Elsa sitting on the carpetbags, ready to fall into the river with any jolt of the boat. "But some people *do* have more privileges than others," Libby answered.

The minute the words were out, Libby felt sorry she had spoken. "I mean, some people are born with more privileges."

"You mean people like you?" Caleb asked.

Libby felt the warm flush of embarrassment creep into her cheeks. Caleb's words cut deep. She wished she could throw them back like a pie in his face.

Instead, she lifted her head, tossing her red curls. "I *like* being the captain's daughter. Is it wrong to appreciate the way you're born?"

Libby's voice trembled. "Is it wrong to appreciate the father you have?"

Now it was Caleb who looked embarrassed. He glanced toward Captain Norstad. "I put my foot into it, didn't I?"

"Yes, Caleb, you did. What do you want to do with your foot?"

His usual confidence gone, Caleb spoke quietly. "I'm sorry, Libby. I'm glad for the way you feel about your pa."

Quick tears welled up in Libby's eyes. Seeing them, Caleb spoke again. "Forgive me?"

Libby hesitated, then glanced toward Pa. His thoughtful eyes watched them both. Knowing she had no choice, Libby nodded.

"What if someone is born into a family who has everything?" Captain Norstad asked.

Again Libby felt uncomfortable. While Pa wasn't wealthy like Auntie Vi, Libby always had everything she needed and more.

Pa seemed to know what she was thinking, for he waited. "Libby?" he asked finally when she did not speak.

Libby shook her head and looked down. With her hands in her lap, she twisted a gold ring Auntie Vi had given her. The morning sun caught the birthstone in its light.

In the silence that filled the room, Libby felt even more uncomfortable. She knew what Pa wanted her to say. A person with many privileges should be wise about how she used them. But Libby was uneasy now, afraid to speak in front of Caleb.

Pa seemed to sense that, for he said, "Let's go back to the Dred Scott decision. If we make another human being a slave, it's like saying, 'You can't work and grow and become all that you have the ability to be.' "

"Oh!" In that moment Libby understood. "That's why it's different for Elsa! Living on the deck is hard for them now, and I know you don't want that, Pa. But when they get to Minnesota Territory, they'll have a home and a farm and grow all the food they need."

"Instead of the life Jordan had as a slave," Caleb said. "Instead of the life he'll have if Riggs finds him."

Captain Norstad nodded. "Go on with the Declaration of Independence, Libby. 'That all men are created equal—' "

Libby took it up. " 'That they are endowed by their Creator'—that their Creator gives them—'certain unalienable Rights, that among these are Life, Liberty and the pursuit of Happiness.' "

"When our founding fathers signed those words, they knew they'd have to fight for them," Pa said. "For your assignment, think about the kind of courage that offers life, liberty, and the pursuit of happiness to every person. Think about ways you can put courage into practice."

Leaving the newspaper open on the table, Captain Norstad stood up and walked out of the room.

The minute the door closed behind him, Libby let out a frustrated sigh. "Do you ever get the feeling that Pa's assignments are *hard*?"

Caleb sat there, tapping a pen against the table and staring off into space. Then he grinned. "I've decided what to do. It will help Jordan and me with our plan to reach his mother."

"Oh, fine!" Libby answered. "Just that quick, you know!"

"Yup." Caleb looked as satisfied as a cat licking his whiskers. "We'll be in Keokuk soon. I'll go into town and ask directions on how to get to the farm where Jordan's mother is."

Feeling even more frustrated, Libby picked up her books. Just before she reached the door, Caleb spoke again.

"Libby, you have every right to feel proud of your pa. He has a good name."

A good name, Libby thought. *What does that mean?* Once again she was too embarrassed to ask.

8

The Great Chase

*L*ater that morning Libby stood high in the pilot-house. Like an arrow the bow of the *Christina* pointed upstream. Behind the boat the wake streamed out like an ever-widening triangle.

Ahead of them, the town of Keokuk, Iowa, rose in a high, rounded bluff. Located at a bend in the river with water flowing to the south and east, the bluff almost looked like an island.

As the *Christina* tied up at the landing, Libby raced out of the pilothouse. By the time she reached Caleb on the main deck, she was out of breath.

"Can I go with you?" she asked.

"If you behave." Caleb grinned.

"I can do that." Libby lowered her voice. "What about Jordan?"

"I asked him to stay on the boat. We're too close to northeastern Missouri where his mother lives. Riggs knows Jordan could try to see his mother."

As soon as the first-class passengers went down the gangplank, Caleb followed them. Libby was only a few steps behind.

When he reached a pile of freight, Caleb looked back. A large crate moved toward them on the shoulder of a tall young man. Whoever carried it had his head down so that Libby saw only the top of his cap.

"Jordan?" Libby whispered.

Caleb's nod was so slight that Libby almost missed it. "I didn't think he'd listen to me."

"Maybe he wants to be courageous," Libby said softly.

"Jordan has plenty of courage," Caleb answered. "But right now, he's being foolhardy!"

"Foolhardy?" Libby asked.

"Reckless. Foolishly bold. Acting before he thinks."

As Libby watched, Jordan set down the crate and started up the steep main street of Keokuk. Acting as if he didn't know Jordan, Caleb strolled after him.

Wandering from one place of business to the next, Caleb looked as if he didn't have a care in the world. Yet he always kept a sharp eye toward wherever Jordan was.

More than once, Libby saw people she recognized as passengers from the *Christina*. One of them was Doctor Fenton, the man who had boarded at St. Louis. In the hours since leaving the city, the *Christina* had made several longer-than-usual stops. Libby hadn't managed to spot the man she felt sure was Riggs. Right now, with Jordan so close by, she felt relieved that Riggs wasn't anywhere in sight.

When Caleb came to a printing office, he led Libby inside. She was surprised to find only one person there—a man named Orion Clemens.

"Any maps for sale?" Caleb asked him.

"Maps?" The man shook his head. "Nope. But we printed the first Keokuk City Directory. Can you use that?"

"Can you give me directions instead?" Caleb named a town across the Iowa border in northeastern Missouri.

Going to the door, Mr. Clemens stepped outside and pointed. "See the red arrow on that tree? Follow that till you see the next arrow, and the next, and the next. Down the road a piece, you'll find a tree with one arrow going straight and another hanging left. Take the arrow hanging left and keep traveling till you see the place you want. You won't miss it."

"Thanks, mister," Caleb answered.

"Anything else I can do for you? You come in on a steamboat?"

"Yup," Caleb said.

"My brother Sam is on the river learning to be a pilot. If you ever see him, give him a howdy."

"Sure thing, mister."

When Caleb and Libby started back to the *Christina*, she saw Jordan leaning against a tree. As Caleb passed him, both he and Jordan acted as if they didn't know each other. Yet when Libby glanced around, Jordan followed a short distance behind.

Just then Libby heard the *Christina*'s deep-throated warning whistle—one long, two short, and one long. "They're ready to board again," she said.

As Caleb picked up his pace, Libby saw a group of older boys around a notice nailed to a building. Some of the tough-looking fellows seemed familiar. With growing uneasiness Libby understood why. She felt sure they were passengers on the *Christina*.

"Look!" a tall blond fellow said. "That's a mighty big reward!"

Libby's uneasiness changed to fear. Strong and rowdy looking, the fellow was probably nineteen or twenty years old. Next to him stood another fellow of about the same age. With dark brown hair, he, too, looked like a bully ready to fight.

Sure that she knew what she'd find, Libby edged forward to read the poster. The words jumped out at her.

$200.00 Reward.

Runaway,

a black boy named

JORDAN PARKER,

about 13 or 14 years of age,

five feet, eleven inches, or six feet tall,

last seen wearing tattered cotton shirt.

Strongly built, walks with head high and a

proud air. . . .

"Two hundred dollars!" the blond bully exclaimed. "What I

could do with that kind of money!"

Trying to not show her fear, Libby stepped back and looked for Caleb. Not far behind her, he, too, had turned. Now he edged out farther into the street. As though nothing important were happening, he stood there, waiting.

Walking on the other side, Jordan drew close. When Caleb's gaze met his, Caleb glanced toward the bullies.

Jordan's head jerked up. As if suddenly aware of danger, his eyes widened. Yet he walked on without changing his pace.

What do I do? thought Libby, then knew she had to pretend nothing was wrong. Walking on her own side of the street, she started after Jordan. She had almost caught up when she heard a shout from behind.

"There he is!" came the cry. "See that proud look? We'll take care of him!"

Libby whirled around. The bully with brown hair pointed down the hill toward Jordan.

"That's him, all right!" another fellow called out.

In the next instant, Jordan broke into a run. At the first break in the line of buildings, he darted between two of them. Reaching a high board fence, he put his hands on top, flipped over, and disappeared.

Libby stared back up the street. Shouting and waving their arms, the gang of bullies raced toward her. As though part of the pack, Caleb joined them.

As the bullies drew close to Libby, Caleb shouted loudly, "Which way did he go?"

"That way!" The blond bully pointed toward the fence.

Caleb pointed in the opposite direction. "Go that way!"

With a burst of speed, Caleb took the lead. Still running like a pack, the gang followed him. Between tall warehouses they raced with Caleb urging them on.

Filled with terror, Libby stared after them. When the bullies came back, they would surely search where Jordan had disappeared.

Slowly Libby turned. She hardly dared look, but when she

did, she saw fingers grasp the top of the fence. Suddenly Jordan leaped back over, landing in the street across from where Libby stood.

Staying close to the buildings, Jordan once again headed toward the *Christina*.

Jordan! Libby wanted to cry out. *You're not safe yet!* But just then a man spoke from directly behind her.

Libby gasped. Her heart pounded with fright.

"Good day, Miss Libby," Doctor Fenton said. Above his salt-and-pepper beard, his cheeks were ruddy. He looked over the glasses perched halfway down his nose.

"You know my name?" Libby asked.

"I understand you're Captain Norstad's daughter."

"Why, yes, I am." Libby felt pleased that he knew.

Politely the doctor tipped his hat. "Are you here by yourself?" he asked with concern. "My friends and I can see you safely back to the boat." He glanced toward the two women walking with him.

"Thank you, sir," Libby said quickly. "I'll be all right." *But I'm sure glad you're not Riggs*, she thought.

"Are you certain?" The doctor's voice was kind. "It seemed there was some kind of ruckus."

"Yes." Libby steadied her voice. "A slight commotion."

"A runaway slave, you think?" the doctor asked. "If so, I hope the fugitive got away."

Libby breathed deeply. *Ahhh! The doctor is on our side!* How good it felt, knowing that.

Libby opened her mouth, ready to tell him. Instead, she heard the warning from the large bell on the *Christina*'s roof. As she listened, Libby counted five taps of the clapper, a space, five more taps, another space, and a final five taps.

"Fifteen minutes," she said. "We need to hurry. If we don't get back, the boat will leave without us."

When the doctor would have waited for her, she told him to go ahead. "I'm meeting a friend," she said. "We'll catch up."

As Doctor Fenton and the two ladies once more started down

the hill, Libby stared after them. Gazing up and down the street, she felt frantic. *Where's Jordan?*

Quickly she ran to the fence and looked over. *Not there. But where is he?*

As the ten-minute warning bell rang, Libby's panic grew. She had no choice but to follow Doctor Fenton. When she was halfway down the hill, she heard the gang of bullies returning. They were still running.

Dividing into two groups, they raced up and down both sides of the street on which Libby walked. At each opening, the bullies ran between buildings, looked around, and returned. When the tall blond fellow reached an open shed, he stopped, peered inside, then hurried on.

"Let's try that other street!" Caleb called, pointing off in another direction. Once again the boys turned to follow him.

Desperately Libby looked around. As she stood there, wondering what to do, a tiny little lady walked up to her.

"Friend," she said, "do you need some help?"

Not sure how to answer, Libby stared at her. "Do you live here?" she asked finally.

The woman smiled. "For many years. And I know how to help you. Look in that shed for your friend." Tipping her head, she nodded across the street.

Without another word the woman disappeared into a nearby building. Quickly Libby crossed the street. As she started past the shed, she heard a whisper.

"Libby!"

Stopping dead in her tracks, she listened.

"Libby!" came the voice again.

It was Jordan, all right, but where was he?

Glancing around, Libby made sure that no one was watching. Then she peered into the shed. A number of big crates were stacked high.

Slowly Libby walked into the shed and around the crates. She couldn't see anyone. "Where are you?" she asked softly.

"Be it safe?" came the whisper back.

This time Libby looked up. The shadow from the roof fell across the uppermost crates. As her eyes grew used to the dim light, she saw Jordan lying on the top crate.

"Just a minute." Returning to the street, Libby gazed up and down. For now all the bullies were gone.

"Hurry!" she said.

With one quick movement, Jordan was off the crate and racing down the street.

Shortly before Libby reached the waterfront, she found another notice. Ripping it down, she stuffed the paper into a pocket and kept walking.

Ahead of her she saw Jordan. When he drew close to the *Christina*, he picked up a barrel. Balancing it on his shoulder, he tipped his head to hide his face and walked up the gangplank. A moment later he disappeared.

As Libby started up the gangplank, Caleb caught up. "Meet us in the captain's cabin," he said in a low voice. Then he, too, disappeared.

9

Free Eyes

*T*en minutes later Libby entered Pa's cabin at the front of the texas deck. When the two boys came in, Libby pulled out the notice she had ripped down. "Here's what caused all the trouble!"

When she laid the paper on the table, Jordan glanced at it, then turned away.

"Look at it!" Libby said.

"I did." Jordan was gazing at the floor.

"Read it!" Libby pointed to the words.

Again Jordan stared at the paper. Pain stole over his face. Once more he looked away.

"I can't," he said.

"Sure, you can," Libby answered.

"Libby," Caleb said softly. "Jordan is trying to tell you something."

But Libby pushed the paper closer to Jordan. "They're still offering two hundred dollars to whoever catches you."

"Stop it, Libby," Caleb said, as though trying to warn her.

Libby paid no attention. "See, Jordan? Read for yourself."

"I can't, Libby," Jordan said again. "I can't read for myself."

This time his quiet words got through. "But, Jordan," Libby stumbled over her words. "Everyone your age knows how to read."

"Everyone but us colored folks." Jordan's head was bowed again, his voice filled with pain. "We ain't allowed to read."

"You aren't allowed to read?" Libby couldn't imagine a life without books.

"And we can't learn to write." Suddenly Jordan lifted his head. "If we knows how, we could write our own passes."

"Passes?" Again Libby felt lost.

"Both slaves and free colored people have to carry a pass," Caleb explained. "Without that piece of paper, they can't travel around alone."

"But I thought—" Libby remembered back. "That time in Pa's cabin when Jordan bent over the map as though reading. And before that, in St. Louis."

She stared at Caleb. "The first time we saw Jordan, you wrote in the dirt. You started writing the *Christina*'s name. When I asked you about it, you said—"

"That I hoped Jordan would remember the letters, and it would help him find the boat."

Finally Libby understood. "Because he couldn't hear the name and know how it would look in writing."

Libby felt embarrassed. "I'm sorry, Jordan. I didn't know."

"I wants to read, Libby," he said. "With all my heart I wants to read the Good Book."

"The Good Book?" Again Libby felt puzzled.

"The Bible," Caleb explained.

"And I wants to read the newspaper like Captain Norstad. I wants to read any book I set my hand on."

Jordan looked from Libby to Caleb. "If I knows how to write my own pass, it be easy to go where my momma is. But I ain't never had no teacher."

"Caleb and I will teach you!" Libby glanced toward Caleb and saw him nod. Turning back to Jordan, Libby saw that a light had come into his face—a light that shone as brightly as the sun.

He pointed out a window. "Look!"

Without their noticing, the *Christina* had put out from Keokuk. In a town a few miles above Keokuk, a small log school stood high on the riverbank. As though on recess, children played in the school yard.

"I could learn like them?" Jordan asked, his voice filled with awe. "I could learn to read a book?"

"You can learn to read like them," Caleb said.

Jordan straightened. Drawing back his shoulders, he held his head high. "I can learn to write?"

"You can learn to write. I promise you," Caleb said. "We'll ask Libby's pa what to do—what books to use."

Libby sat down at the table. "Let's start with the alphabet right now. When you know the letters, you can put them together into words."

Taking up a slate, she wrote a letter. "*A*," she said, printing it as she spoke. "*A* is for apple."

Caleb handed Jordan another slate. "Make the letter after Libby."

When she reached the letter *L*, Libby stopped. "That's enough for today."

"That's all the alphabet?" Jordan asked.

"No," Libby answered. "But I don't want to mix you up by giving too much at once."

"I want to know *all* the alphabet," Jordan said, unwilling to stop.

Then Libby saw what Caleb was doing. With a pen he had written each letter on a paper Jordan could keep.

"*L* is for Libby," she said, and Jordan grinned.

From one letter to the next she went, with Jordan carefully copying her printing.

Before long, Libby wrote an *R*. "*R* is for Riggs," she said, expecting another grin. Instead, Jordan's hand started to tremble.

"What's the matter, Jordan?" Caleb asked.

As though telling them to pay no attention, Jordan shook his head. But when Libby started an *S*, Jordan stopped her. "After we left St. Louis last night, I seen a man on this boat," he said. "A man that looks a powerful lot like Riggs."

"Did he have a handlebar mustache?" Libby blurted out.

"I only seen his back and the side of his head," Jordan answered. "He were short and skinny just like Riggs. He gots a cane with gold on it."

"Libby thinks she saw Riggs come on board in St. Louis," Caleb said. "If he did, his name isn't on the passenger list. I haven't been able to find out what room he's in."

Jordan's dark eyes widened with fear. "I ain't got no likin' for being near that man!"

"If Riggs is a first-class passenger—and he must be—stay off the boiler deck," Caleb warned. "That's where he'd spend most of his time."

"But there's something else," Libby said. "You know those bullies who chased you, Jordan? I've seen them on the *Christina*."

"Are they deckers or first-class passengers?" Caleb asked.

Libby thought about it. "Probably deckers."

Jordan groaned. "So what does I do?"

"Could you stay in the engine room, like Pa said you should when we're in port?" Libby asked.

"But Captain Norstad, he give me a *job*! He *pays* me to take care of his clothes and run his errands. How can I do my work?"

"I'll help with Pa's clothes," Libby said quickly.

Caleb shook his head. "Jordan, you should keep off both the boiler deck and the main deck. If you stay up here on the texas deck, you can do your work and have classes. I'll bring you food."

Seeming to know that he had no choice, Jordan agreed to that. Yet they still had the problem of finding Riggs somewhere among the three hundred people on board. Libby knew they needed all the help they could get.

"Jordan, you haven't told me how you got away when Riggs was your master," she said. "Would you mind telling me now? Maybe if we knew more about him, it would help us find Riggs."

"Where does I start?" Jordan asked.

"With the auction," Libby said.

As though feeling the pain of that terrible day, Jordan's eyes grew wet with tears. He turned to Caleb. "When you was at the auction, what you did gave me hope."

Jordan pointed to his chest. "In here I tells myself, 'Jordan, if a white boy cares what happens to you, you better pay attention.'"

Jordan swallowed hard. "Long time ago my daddy and my momma had a good master. One that treated them mighty fine. Like members of the family they was. They work in the Big House just like they belong.

"My momma were a mammy for the master's children. But then the master fell on hard times. My momma and my daddy and my sisters and my brother and me was sold to Old Massa."

"An old master?" Libby asked, and Jordan nodded.

"I was just so high." Jordan put out his hand about three feet above the floor. "That's when my daddy said to me, 'Jordan, I hope you always gits a good master. But if you git a bad one, look up at the sky and follow the North Star. Before your master knows what's in your head, run for your life. The longer you with a cruel master, the harder it be to git away.'

"Once before I minded my daddy's words. I run, but the slave catchers brung me back. When that slave trader Riggs put me in his wagon, I thinks, 'Jordan, you gots yourself a cruel master again. But that white boy wants to help you. You gots to find him real fast.'

"So I watched the road we take. I watched the way we go. As I watched I tell myself, 'Jordan, you got this one licked. You know where you is.'"

"You *knew*?" Libby asked.

"Yes'm. After Old Massa sold my daddy away, he took me to the big city. Wanted to buy a new stove, he did, and took me along. Everywhere I went, I watched and I listened. One day my listenin' paid off. Old Massa took me to a house where a free colored man sells stoves.

"When Old Massa turned his back, the stove man stepped real close. He spoke low in my ear. 'You want your freedom?'

"I nodded my head like it was going to shake off. 'When you gits your chance you come here,' the man said. 'All you gots to say is "My massa needs a new stove."'

"Old Massa took me away then. When I gits home, I tell my momma what the stove man said. Momma said, 'We is goin' to run, Jordan. We gots to run before Old Massa pulls my children from my arms.'

"While I tries to find a way, Old Massa sell Momma and my sisters and my brother. Sells them up north from where I was. Then Old Massa dies."

"And you were sold to Riggs?" Libby asked.

"Yes'm. After the auction I sits in the back of the wagon and looks at Riggs. I thinks, 'Jordan, your leg-irons keep your feets from running. But your eyes is free. You let those eyes tell you where you is.'

"So I watch the streets and houses. I knows when we goes near that stove-buying place. I fix in my mind the way to go back."

"And then?" Libby asked as Jordan paused. "What happened next?"

"Riggs, he stopped at a big house and climbed down. I thinks, 'This is where he lives?' But when he walks up to the door, a dog come rushing at him. A little bitty dog with legs like sticks and a bark as scary as a baby's cry."

Jordan barked a timid little woof that made Libby giggle.

"But that Riggs, he backs away, as scared as you please. Climbed into the wagon like he was going to lose a leg!"

Again Libby giggled.

"When we gits to his house, Riggs drove his wagon into his barn. My eyes is still workin' to be free. I looks around for a way to escape. I sees a work bench and tools along one wall. Then Riggs drags me out of the wagon, tells me to stand up like a man, and takes out a whip."

"You don't have to tell her," Caleb said quickly. "Libby saw your back."

Libby remembered the torn flesh. The deep marks from a whip laid one way, then another. Jordan would wear those scars the rest of his life.

Now his fingers tightened into fists. " 'I gots a cruel master,' I thinks again as Riggs lays the whip down hard. When he done, Riggs throws me into the next room and lock the door.

"As I lies there, I remembers my daddy again. 'Jordan, if you git a cruel master, you escape fast.' I thinks, 'Soon it be night, and I can't see.' So I remembers the tools in the next room. I thinks, 'I gots to git to 'em. That's my only way out.'

"My prison were a small room built so tight it look like a place for storing grain," Jordan said. "Not a window there. Not even a crack big enough to let in a mouse.

"So I thinks, 'No window. Why is I seein' anything at all?' I looks up and, sure enough, I see light comin' through a hole in the ceiling. It weren't a big hole. Not big enough for a man to go through. But could I?

"I see a ladder nailed to the wall going up to the hole. But Riggs, he took care of that ladder too. Halfway up the wall, that ladder be sawed off.

"So I ask myself, 'How you goin' to reach that ladder, Jordan?' And I think on it. I think, 'If I put my hands behind my back at about my waist—' He showed them. 'And if I lean into the wall, real hard—' "

"On your back?" Libby was horrified. "It was raw and bleeding!"

"Yes'm. Tried not to touch my back, but I did. I pressed into the wall on one side. The room were so small I walked up the wall on the other side."

"Are you serious?" Libby couldn't believe it. "You *walked* right up the wall? You had leg-irons on!"

"Yes'm. I swung my legs this way and that and jiggled myself till I reached the ladder. Pulled myself through that little hole and dropped down into the room where the tools was kept.

"It was gittin' dark now, and I knows I has to hurry. Looked through all the tools till I found a cold chisel and a hammer."

Jordan grinned. "That were the easiest part of gittin' away. One smack on that chain between my legs and it broke. Quick as a wink, I found an old rag, tore it in strips. Pulled up my pant legs and tied the rest of the chain to my legs."

"And your pant legs covered your leg-irons so no one could see you were wearing them," Libby said.

Jordan nodded. "By now it were dark. I goes to the door and takes a look. I slips through and shuts that door behind me.

"Just then I hears someone coming. He was whistling as happy as a lark. But my heart was shivering. I knows it be Riggs, and I remembers what he said when he bought me. 'No slave ever got away from me—alive, that is!' "

10

Shivery Heart

*L*ibby's heart shivered too. Just hearing about the evil slave trader scared her. "Go on, Jordan," she said.

"Fast as a cat on a hot tin roof I run for the bushes and gits down behind them. I knows that if Riggs finds me, I sure enough git another beating. When he comes round the corner, my heart pounds out of my chest." As though feeling the fear again, Jordan's eyes widened.

"What did you do?" Libby asked.

"I barked."

"You *barked*?"

Jordan laughed. "Like this." As though he were the most savage dog on earth, he growled and snarled.

Just listening to him, Libby felt afraid. "If I didn't see you right in front of me, I wouldn't believe it was you."

Jordan grinned. "Riggs was so skeered of my bark that he didn't go into the barn. When he goes back to the house, I runs away.

"I ain't got no pass, so I hides behind trees and bushes. I sneaks along in the dark till I finds the free colored man who sells stoves. He take one look at me and said, 'You shore took a long time in comin'. I is mighty glad you're here.'

"When I told him my story, he said, 'You trust that white boy?'

" 'I trusts that boy,' I said.

" 'Then I need to deliver a stove up that way,' he said. 'I take you to him, and if he ain't there, I know another way.' "

"Through Alton, Illinois?" Caleb asked.

Jordan nodded. "Next morning that stove man hide me in a crate in his wagon. Then he puts in another crate with a great big stove. On the way, men stop us. That stove man said, 'Here my pass.' They checked the crate closest to the back end of the wagon. Then they said, 'Go on, boy. Guess we're lookin' for someone else.'

"When no one there, that stove man talk to me. 'We be goin' on a ferry now,' he said once. After we drive and drive and drive, he said, 'Now we wait for dark.'

"When night comes, he opens my crate. I looks and waits. No houses there, just trees and bushes. The moon and stars shows me where I is. I sees a river so big I knows I is crossin' into the Promised Land."

"Across the Mississippi and into the free state of Illinois," Libby said.

Jordan's eyes shone with the memory. "When a cloud passes over the moon, a girl comes out of the bushes. 'You ready?' I hears her whisper. Then I see a rowboat and two boys. They show me how to lie down in the boat. They put a heavy cloth over me and cover up everything but my face.

"While one boy rowed, another put out a line to fish. 'We'll bring you close to a tunnel,' he said. 'When we come to shore, you run straight ahead as fast as you can.'

"I wants to find the *Christina*,' I tells them.

" 'The *Christina*?' That boy sure was surprised. But the other boy said, 'We'll bring you where the steamboats take on wood.'

"When we gits close to the shore, those boys cover my face. Soon I feels the boat bump against something. 'This is Alton,' one of them said. 'We're at a flat rock—a stone wharf. When we lift the cover, step out on the wharf as though you belong here. Walk straight ahead as though you know what you're doing. When you see a woodpile, look for a tall man with a beard. He'll tell you what to do.'

"I found that tall man with a beard," Jordan said simply, as though his story had come to a close. "When I said, 'The *Christina*,' he acted like he knew you, Caleb. He hide me between the piles of wood till it was time to go on board."

"We're going to get your momma out," Caleb promised as he had before. "There's one thing we know from going into Keokuk. Your proud look gives you away."

"My proud look?" Jordan asked, as if he didn't know what Caleb meant.

Libby picked up the wanted poster she had torn down. "It's right here." Even when Jordan was being sold as a slave, he had reminded Libby of royalty. She read the words describing him:

Strongly built, walks with head high and a proud air. . . .

"Either we have to travel at night, or you have to wear a disguise," Caleb told Jordan.

"You, too, Caleb," Libby reminded him. "Slave catchers know you. If you're recognized, you'll give Jordan away."

Caleb ran his fingers through his blond hair, as though trying to think what to do. "First we have to keep you safe, Jordan, no matter what Riggs tries to do."

"If that man I seen last night was Riggs, why didn't he grab me then?" Jordan asked.

"Because he's watching all of us," Caleb answered. "He wants to know what we're doing, who we take on, how we do it. When he knows that and how to catch Libby's pa, Riggs will make his move."

Libby groaned. "Caleb, how can you say such a terrible thing?"

"Because we have to know what we're up against. If we don't, Riggs will catch us for sure."

Then teasing lit Caleb's eyes. "It's all up to you, Libby. You're the one who eats in the main cabin. Maybe you'll spot Riggs there."

Libby felt nervous just thinking about it. Pulling forward a long, red curl, she twisted it between her fingers. Soon she had it all tangled up, but she didn't feel any better.

❀

When they stopped in Burlington, Libby saw Caleb hurry down the gangplank and disappear. When he returned, Caleb looked pleased with himself.

Soon after, Libby noticed Caleb and Jordan together. But to Libby, Caleb said only, "Jordan and I have figured out how we can get to where his mother is."

"What do you mean?" Libby asked.

"You'll see," Caleb answered.

During the evening meal, Libby searched for Riggs. The large cabin that served as a dining room stretched from one end of the boat to the other. Captain Norstad sat at the front of the cabin with his officers.

Sitting next to her father, Libby ate with only half her attention on her food. With each forkful she thought about Elsa and how much she would like a meal like this. Taking one table at a time, Libby looked around for Riggs.

Again she passed over the women and the tall men, searching for someone short and slender. *But Riggs could wear padding*, she reminded herself. *He might look heavier.*

As Libby watched, talk about the upcoming race swirled around her.

"What's the news from Reads Landing?" asked Mr. Bates, the first mate. The busy steamboat stop lay at the foot of Lake Pepin.

"Minnesota Territory has had the worst winter in years," Captain Norstad answered. "They've had four feet of snow on the ground. When the wind picked up, drifts covered houses and barns."

"And Lake Pepin?" asked Osborne, the chief engineer. Pepin was a widening in the Mississippi River as it flowed between Minnesota Territory and the state of Wisconsin.

"The lake is still frozen over," Captain Norstad answered. "Every day more boats arrive at Reads Landing. We'll have a fine race this year."

Libby glanced around the table. Each man looked eager for the big event that opened the 1857 season. The race through Lake Pepin was exciting. The first steamboat through the ice-filled waters won the honor of first arrival in St. Paul. Yet the race was also dangerous. Every spring some boats were wrecked trying to get through Lake Pepin.

Now Captain Norstad held out the bait—a sizable reward offered by the city of St. Paul. "Whoever wins the race won't have to pay a cent all season for using their wharf."

"We'll do it, all right!" Osborne grinned, as though thinking about all the ways he could pour on steam.

Bates looked just as eager. "If we're first, we'll have even more passengers and freight."

"We'll reach Reads Landing on time?" That was young Martin, the mud clerk. "Before the ice goes out?"

No one else would even think of asking such a question. Of course they would make it there on time.

"We won't miss the opening of the season," Captain Norstad answered, making no mention of the newspapers or the telegraph reports he checked daily. "If all goes well, we'll be at Reads Landing in two days. My good friend Daniel Smith Harris might already be there."

"Captain Harris?" young Martin blurted out. "But he's won the race four years in a row!"

"That doesn't mean he'll win the fifth," Captain Norstad said calmly. "But if he does, he's still my friend!"

Libby could hardly wait to reach Reads Landing, to see the famous riverboat captains and be part of the race. But right now she had more things on her mind. As she bit into one of Granny's delicious rolls, Libby turned to see the men at another table. All of them were too tall to be Riggs.

Just then Bates took a large piece of meat, cut off one slice, and left the rest on his plate. Again Libby remembered Elsa. "Please—" Libby spoke before thinking.

When Bates looked up, Libby swallowed her words. Here in the elegant main cabin she couldn't ask for someone else's food. But Libby remembered the Meyer family's celebration. *One herring each. And the one I didn't eat went back in the bottle.*

Libby stared at each plate. Those potatoes, that piece of meat. On deck the people would fall upon those tasty morsels as a meal fit for a king.

Before long the waiter set down thirteen desserts in a circle about Libby's plate. Six of the desserts were served in tall, slender glasses. The other seven were pies, puddings, and ice creams. Each dish was for her alone.

Before Libby would have taken a dainty spoonful from every dish, trying each one. Now she thought about Elsa instead. The Meyer family carried a long tube of smoked sausage in their trunk. Libby had watched Mr. Meyer carefully slice off pieces. Last night only a small piece of sausage remained.

I'll talk to Granny, Libby decided.

Toward the far end of the cabin, there were tables Libby couldn't see. The moment Pa gave her permission to leave, Libby leaped up from her chair. Walking slowly, she studied each of the people she had not seen. Suddenly she spied a gold-headed cane.

Ah! Libby stopped. But the gentleman using it was definitely not Riggs. Libby turned away in disappointment.

Then her keen artist's eye rested on a man whose back was turned to her. His hair was the right color. The way he sat seemed familiar. As Libby watched, he took a mustache cup from the waiter. Whoever the passenger was, he needed the special cup to hold his mustache above his coffee.

Like a cat creeping up on a mouse, Libby walked closer. When she saw the man's face, she felt sure. *Riggs!*

I'll follow him! Libby decided. *I'll find out where his cabin is. Then Caleb can keep an eye on him.*

Moments later the man looked up. As his gaze met Libby's, she felt sure of something else. *I can't stand here watching. He'll know exactly what I'm doing.*

Slowly she walked away. Outside the main door of the cabin, she stopped and glanced back. The man who looked like Riggs was still watching her.

I'll sneak around to another door, Libby decided. But when she reached the door on the side of the cabin, the man was gone!

Libby trembled. *I was so close! In one minute I lost him!* Again she understood what Jordan meant by a shivery heart. *What if the man truly is Riggs, and he's setting a trap for Jordan even now?*

Trying to push aside her fear, Libby decided she would feel better if she talked to Caleb's grandmother.

On her way to the kitchen, Libby ran into Caleb. "I saw Riggs!" she exclaimed. "But I lost him! He caught me looking and must have gone out a different door."

"He was in the dining room?" Caleb asked.

"Using a mustache cup. Is there any reason a man would wear a false mustache if it weren't a disguise?" Libby asked.

Caleb shrugged. "He might want to see if other people like it. But if he looked like Riggs, I'm going to search this whole deck right away. I can go into places where you can't."

Once again Libby headed for the pastry kitchen to find Granny. Samson followed close behind.

Caleb's grandmother had gray-white hair pulled back and twisted into a knot at the top of her head. Smile wrinkles around her eyes made Granny seem young. She took one look at Samson and said, "You can't come into my nice, clean kitchen."

As close to the doorway as he could get, Samson sat down on his haunches. Tipping his head to one side, he watched every move, as though waiting for a tasty scrap to fall.

"Granny, I have a friend," Libby started out.

"A friend among the deckers, and you want food."

Libby stared at her. "How did you know?"

"Because Caleb does the same thing. On every trip he finds a friend. Someone who is starving usually." Already Gran had taken a cloth from the cupboard. Spreading it out on a counter, she began filling it with thick slices of bread and cheese.

"Fruit," she said. "Your friend needs fruit more than anything."

Going to a barrel in the pantry, Granny took an apple—one of the apples Libby barely saw when it was cut up and placed in a design on her plate.

Drawing up the four corners, Granny tied the cloth into a bag and handed it to Libby. "Mind you, be careful," Granny warned. "Don't let the other deckers see what you're doing."

Libby didn't need to be told. Carefully she slipped the bag of food inside her coat and went out on deck. As she drew near to where the Meyer family lived, Libby heard them singing.

Huddled beneath Libby's quilt, Elsa sat on top of the woodpile. Mrs. Meyer made room for Libby on the trunk, while Mr. Meyer stood nearby. Without a break in their music, each of them smiled at Libby.

Today Elsa seemed even more pale. Yet her eyes lit up as she joined her parents in singing one song after another. In spite of the German words, one of the songs seemed familiar to Libby. Then she recognized the tune of "A Mighty Fortress Is Our God." Libby had never heard it sung with as much spirit.

Leaning close to Elsa, Libby slipped her the bag of food.

Surprise flashed across Elsa's face. "Danke, Libby," she said softly. "Thanks so much."

"I need to go now," Libby answered. She wanted to give her friend a chance to eat.

Standing up, Libby started off. She was partway to the next deck when she remembered. *I forgot to tell Elsa that in two days we'll be at Reads Landing.*

Libby started back. When she rounded the corner near the family's space, Libby saw that Elsa had crawled down from the woodpile. Using the trunk as a table, she had opened the cloth and divided the food into three portions.

Quickly Libby backed away. *Next time I need to bring more. Enough for all three of them.*

11

Cinderella

*A*ll the way up to the texas deck, Libby thought about the Meyer family. In spite of their hard life, there was something warm between them—something that brought them together. Elsa's face had lit up as if the words of the hymn meant everything to her. Were they singing hymns to keep up their courage?

Libby couldn't explain her feelings, even to herself. *Always they seem so close*, Libby thought. *They're a real family.*

When she found her father in his cabin, Libby sat down next to him at the large, round table. She told him about Mr. and Mrs. Meyer and Elsa, then said, "I wish we could be a family like that, Pa."

Pa looked at her in surprise. "Libby, we *are* a family like that. Don't you remember telling me that you wanted a never-give-up family?"

Libby remembered all right, but that wasn't what she meant. "I wish Ma were here again. I wish we could laugh and sing and be together."

To Libby's great embarrassment, tears choked off her words.

Deep inside, she still felt a longing for her mother. Sometimes Libby missed her mother as though it were yesterday that Ma died, instead of four years ago.

Reaching out, Pa gathered Libby into his arms. "I miss her, too, Libby. I still ache with missing her. Is that what you're feeling?"

Her head against Pa's chest, Libby nodded.

"Your ma was a very special woman, Libby. One of a kind, just like you."

Leaning back, Libby looked up into her father's eyes. "I'm like Ma?"

"More than I can tell you, Libby."

"How am I like my mother?" Libby was curious now.

"Well, the most obvious thing is your hair. The pretty auburn color—deep red with gold highlights. And your dark brown eyes. But there's much more. There's something about your spirit."

"What's that, Pa?"

"It's the way you look at things. When you get knocked down, you get up again. Remember the first night we were back together?"

Libby nodded. During four long years, she had seen Pa only now and then. Pa had felt that she was too young to live on a riverboat without Ma being there.

Now Pa looked her straight in the eyes. "That's the night you told me, 'Pa, I want a never-give-up family. I want a family that believes in me, even when I'm not perfect.' "

"We're that family?" Libby asked.

"We're that family, even though it's just the two of us. We'll stick together even when it's hard."

"Pa, will you keep telling me about Ma?"

Her father smiled. "Whenever you like. First you need to know her secret codes."

"Ma had secret codes?" Libby asked.

"Remember when you were a runner in St. Louis? I winked at you."

Libby remembered all right. That long, slow wink had made her think, *Pa feels proud of me.*

"That was one of your mother's secret codes. She started winking right after we were married. Sometimes when we were in public, she wanted to tell me, 'I love you.' "

"Ma did?"

"She always found a way to have fun. Once she was across the room, and there was someone in between."

Now Libby remembered. "Ma winked one long wink. A lady named Mrs. Blakely was there."

"A very prim and proper lady," Pa said. "Mrs. Blakely had the most perfect manners of anyone I ever met. Her husband was part owner of the *Christina* then."

"Ma wanted to say 'I love you' in front of *her*?"

Libby's pa started laughing with just the memory of it. "Your ma winked at me. I saw her and winked back. Mrs. Blakely didn't see me, but she noticed your mother. She asked, 'Do you have something in your eye, Mrs. Norstad?'

" 'Why, yes, I'm afraid so,' your mother said. She couldn't say it was love she had in her eye."

Libby giggled. "But the rest of the afternoon, Ma winked at you!"

Suddenly it was desperately important for Libby to know more. "Pa, how else am I like my mother?"

Her father's arm tightened around her. "When you smile, I see her smile. When you laugh, I hear her laugh," Pa said gently. "But you're also your own special person."

"So what do you mean?" Libby asked. "How am I like Ma?"

"In the very hardest times, your mother would lift her head and toss her curls like you do. She'd say, 'We'll go on.' She'd head upstream, even if it was hard."

More than once Libby had stood at the window in the captain's cabin, looking down. Always she liked seeing the bow of the *Christina* cut through water. It wasn't easy going upstream.

Downstream, yes, with the keelboats and rafts that still ran the river when it was free of ice. But people had a hard time going upstream until the steam engine was invented.

"Your mother had courage, Libby. When something went wrong, or in times when I was afraid, she had courage."

Courage is just what I need, Libby thought as she had before. "Pa," she asked, "how did Ma get courage?"

"True courage is given by God," Pa answered simply. "God was important to her."

He could be important to me too, Libby thought. She remembered the words that had seemed so real in the dark hold of the boat. In spite of her terrible fear, that moment had become special. *Is that what it means to know God the way Ma did? The way Pa knows God even now?*

Then Libby pushed her wondering aside. *I don't need God for everyday things. Just when I'm desperate.*

❁

After classes the next morning, Libby took her pencils and paper and went to the area where first-class passengers walked for exercise. While living in Chicago, Libby had taken drawing lessons, and she practiced whenever she could. *Someday I'll be an artist*, Libby told herself. But today there was something else to be concerned about. *If Riggs comes along, I'll see him right away.*

Next to the railing, Libby dropped down on the deck. Here she could look at the scenery along the shore and also watch any passengers. At first Libby sketched the trees they passed. Some of them had the small, bright green leaves of early spring. Then a young girl and her parents came out on the deck.

Soon Libby started drawing the child. One line here, another line there. Before long the little girl took shape. Libby studied her drawing and felt pleased. *Just a few more wispy curls around her face.*

As Libby held the picture at arm's length, the father walked around behind her. "What a good likeness of our daughter!" he told Libby. "Please, can we buy it from you?"

"Buy it?" Libby felt surprised that anyone could be willing to pay for what she had drawn. But the man pulled his wife over to see.

"It's lovely!" she exclaimed. "Do you do this for all the passengers?"

Libby shook her head. "Just special ones. I noticed your daughter playing."

"It looks exactly like her," the mother said. "It would be a lovely keepsake from our trip."

"Please," the father said again. "Let us buy it from you." Digging into a pocket, he felt for his money. "Would this be enough?" he asked as he dropped a small gold coin into Libby's hand.

Enough? Libby stared down at the money. *He wants to pay me all that?*

Pulling her thoughts together, Libby offered the smile she often practiced in front of a mirror. "Thanks, that will be just fine," she answered. "Thank you for liking my drawing."

"Please sign it," the mother said quickly.

How do I do that? Libby wondered. Then from her excited thoughts came the memory of a painting in her teacher's house. Taking up her pencil again, Libby added her name. *Libby Norstad, 1857.*

As she handed the sketch to the mother, a great swelling of joy welled up inside Libby. *I did it! I did it! I did it! I sold a drawing!*

When the family walked away, Libby looked up to find Caleb. She had no idea when he had come on deck. "Did you see that?" Libby asked. "I can't believe it!"

"I can." Caleb's blue eyes shone with excitement. "I saw your drawing, and it was good—really good!"

Hearing his praise, Libby could barely speak. *If Caleb says something, he means it. Maybe I truly will be an artist someday!*

"And you know what?" Caleb asked. "I have a feeling that your drawing ability will help us free Jordan's family. I don't know how, but let's think about it."

Only then did Libby remember. She had been so busy drawing that she forgot to look for Riggs.

❋

When the *Christina* put in at LaCrosse, Wisconsin, Libby invited Elsa to go for a walk. Samson followed them down the gangplank.

Near the place where the Black River and the LaCrosse River flowed into the Mississippi, Libby found a stick and threw it out. "Get it, Samson!"

Leaping into the air, the dog caught it in his mouth. When he brought the stick to Libby, she flung it out again.

Soon Elsa took up the game, throwing out the stick for Samson. Each time he brought it back, he dropped it at Elsa's feet, then waited for her to tell him, "Good dog!"

Wanting to make it harder for Samson, Libby threw the stick farther than ever before. As her throw went wild, the stick landed in the cold, black water of the Mississippi.

Instantly Samson raced after it. At the edge of the river, he gathered his front paws together and dived into the water. Paddling quickly, he reached the stick and caught it up in his mouth.

When he brought the stick to Libby, she laughed. "You sure aren't afraid of water!" This time she deliberately threw it into the river. Again Samson retrieved it, paddling as though he enjoyed the ice-cold water.

"Make it even harder," Caleb said when he joined them. "Samson will like you for it."

Searching along the riverbank, Caleb found part of a branch that had washed up on shore. After showing it to Samson, Caleb flung it far out.

"Why isn't he cold?" Elsa asked as she watched Samson swim.

"He's bred for this," Caleb told her. "Newfies have two coats of hair, the long outer one you see and a shorter inner one."

"What did you call him?" Elsa asked.

"A Newfie. Sea captains keep Newfoundlands on their ships to rescue men if they fall overboard."

Soon Samson returned the branch, laying it at Caleb's feet. For a time Caleb let him swim, and Samson played like a child in the water. At last Caleb's low whistle brought the dog in.

In spite of Elsa's sweater and coat, her lips looked blue with cold. Holding her arms, she hugged herself against the sharp spring wind.

Seeing Elsa's pale cheeks, Libby felt uneasy. "Let's go back," she said. As they traveled north, the cold seemed increasingly hard on her friend. Yet Elsa had no place to get warm. The crowd of deckers always kept her away from the stove in the deck room.

When they reached the Meyers' small space on main deck, Elsa used Libby's quilt to cover her head and shoulders. Only the front of Elsa's blond hair and her too-white face showed. Whenever she spoke, her teeth chattered with cold.

I'll take her to the stove in the main cabin, Libby thought. Then she remembered. That stove was only for first-class passengers.

But Libby pushed the thought aside. *Pa talked about courage. Maybe it's courage to take Elsa there.*

Feeling concerned for her friend, Libby made up her mind. *Elsa is only one person. It's not like I invited all one-hundred-and-fifty deckers.*

"C'mon," Libby said. "I'll take you to the main cabin. There's a stove that will keep you warm."

Elsa hung back. "But, Libby, that's for people who pay full fare."

"So?" Libby asked.

Elsa looked embarrassed now. "We didn't pay full fare. We didn't even pay full deck fare. Father is working his way carrying wood."

"I know, I know." Libby had seen what happened when they came aboard. *I can take Elsa to the main cabin anyway*, she thought. *No one will ever know.*

"Smooth your dress," she told Elsa. "Act like you know what you're doing."

"I don't like it, Libby. I'll be all right here on deck. Your quilt helps a lot."

Without another word Libby started toward the wide steps at the front of the boat. Looking half afraid and half eager, Elsa laid aside the quilt and followed Libby.

Partway up, the broad steps divided into two narrower stairways. Elsa walked on the thick red carpet as though she were Cinderella going to the ball.

When they reached the boiler deck, Libby opened the double doors into the main cabin. She had grown used to the cabin's unusual beauty, but Elsa stood in the doorway, her eyes wide with awe.

"This one room is almost as long as the whole boat!" she exclaimed.

Now, between meals, the large dining room was divided in its use. On a carpeted section at one end, a group of women sat in a circle talking. Unless invited into the women's half, men were expected to stay at the other end. Instead of carpeting, their section had a wood floor for the men who missed the spittoon when spitting tobacco.

Large oil paintings hung on the long sides of the cabin. Like a moth attracted to light, Elsa was drawn to them.

"Here," Libby said quickly, trying to steer her friend to the stove in the women's section.

But Elsa had forgotten about getting warm. Paying no attention to Libby, she headed for the nearest painting.

Standing beneath the first one, Elsa stared up at it. "Ohhh!" she said, barely breathing.

When she moved on to the second painting, she again stood beneath it, gazing upward. "Beautiful! Beautiful!" she exclaimed, her words heavy with a German accent.

Just then Libby saw a woman looking at Elsa. Leaning forward, she touched the arm of another woman. When both of them turned to watch Elsa, Libby knew she was in trouble.

"Elsa!" Libby spoke in a low voice. "Forget the paintings. Go stand by the stove."

Instead, Elsa hurried on. As she gazed up at the next painting, Libby saw the second woman poke a third, then a fourth. Soon the entire group of women was watching Elsa.

When she turned to Libby, Elsa saw the women. A red flush spread across her face. "Let's go, Libby," she whispered.

Libby was glad to leave, but it was too late. Just then Mr. Bates passed through on the walkway between the men's and women's sections. One of the women motioned to the first mate. Though Libby could not hear, she had no doubt what was being said.

With Elsa close behind, Libby walked as fast as she dared toward the large main door. Bates caught up with her there.

"So, Miss Libby," he said. "Do you think you can break the rules just because you're the captain's daughter?"

Elsa's flush deepened. *She understands*, Libby thought, and that shamed her even more.

Without either of them speaking, Libby and Elsa hurried down the red carpeted steps. After the beauty of the main cabin, the dirt and crowding on the main deck seemed even worse.

I guess that wasn't courage, Libby thought. *Now that Elsa knows how first-class passengers live, being a decker will be even worse.*

Then Libby had an idea.

12

Green-Eyed Caterpillar

"*I*'m going to ask Pa if Elsa can have lessons with Caleb and me," Libby told Granny the next morning. "In Pa's cabin she'll be warm at least part of the day."

Then it dawned on Libby. "Elsa reads German. How do I teach her English?"

"Start the way you did with Jordan," Granny said. "Be sure she knows the English alphabet."

Once again Libby gathered up food and tucked it inside her coat. "Thanks, Granny," she said. Bending down, she dropped a quick kiss on the older woman's cheek.

When Libby delivered the food, she sat down to talk. "Every day Caleb and I have school together," she told Elsa. "My pa teaches us. Would you like to have class with us?"

This time Elsa was on guard about Libby's idea. No more going where she wasn't wanted just because it was warm. Not for Elsa. Her pride was too great.

Pride? Libby wondered. Or an *independent spirit?* Whatever it was, Libby didn't want to destroy it.

"Is all right with your father, the captain?" Elsa asked carefully.

"Pa says, 'Invite Elsa to school. If she wants to learn, we will teach her to read and write English.'"

"English?" A smile broke across Elsa's pale face. Turning to her parents, she spoke rapidly in German.

Mr. Meyer listened, then nodded. "You go. In America you must know more English."

"Yah." Even Mrs. Meyer seemed to understand. "You teach it to us."

As Libby led her friend from the crowded space, Elsa's hand felt cold to the touch. But her face glowed with excitement.

When they reached Captain Norstad's cabin, he was not yet there. Caleb sat with Jordan along one side of the table. Libby and Elsa sat down across from them.

Elsa already knew the English alphabet well. As Libby wondered what to do next, she listened to Caleb. He pointed to Samson lying outside the door.

"Dog," Caleb said. He sounded the *d*. "D-d-d. Da-og. Dog."

Carefully he printed the letters. On another slate Jordan copied the word.

In that moment Libby decided what to try. For Elsa she drew a picture of Caleb, then pointed to him. "Boy. B-b-b. B-oy."

"Boy," Elsa repeated, then copied Libby's printing.

Soon Libby began drawing more difficult ideas—her father with his captain's hat on. "Captain," she printed.

When Caleb kept teaching easy words, Jordan stopped him. "I wants to write my name."

Caleb sounded out Jordan, then printed it.

As soon as Jordan could write his first name, he wanted to know how to write his last name, Parker. Again Caleb showed him.

When Jordan finished printing, he held up his slate. With great pride he showed them what he had done. "Jordan Parker," he read aloud, as though unable to believe what he saw.

Suddenly he laughed. "I wish my daddy and my momma could see me now!"

Caught up in his excitement, Elsa laughed too. The happy sound warmed Libby.

I did a good thing by bringing Elsa here, she thought. *That must be the kind of courage Pa means.*

But just then Caleb looked across the table at Elsa. As though seeing her for the first time, Caleb studied Elsa's face.

In spite of being too thin, she had a special kind of beauty. Here, where she was not chattering with cold, Libby saw her white-blond hair and deep blue eyes in a new way.

"You are free now?" Elsa asked Jordan.

Jordan stiffened. He glanced at Caleb, as though wondering what to say. Caleb answered for him.

"Elsa, what does your family believe about slavery?"

"My father says 'No man should be slave!'" Pretending she was Mr. Meyer, Elsa slammed her hand on the table. "'*Ach!*' he says. 'No man should be unfairly treated!'"

Elsa's blue eyes sparkled with laughter. "So!" She spoke directly to Jordan. "Are you afraid to tell me that you have run away?"

Jordan's gaze met hers. "I ain't afraid to tell you, but I'm wishin' you don't have to know."

"In my country—" Elsa shrugged as if she, too, knew what it meant to be poor and unfairly treated. "My family left it behind. We have hope for something better."

Caleb leaned forward. "Elsa, when your family gets to Minnesota Territory, where will you live?"

"My father wants to find land near Red—" Elsa paused as if wanting to make sure of the name.

"Red Wing," Caleb said quickly. "A town above Lake Pepin. Then we'll see you again. After you get off the boat, I mean. The *Christina* often stops at Red Wing."

Oh, it does, does it? A feeling of dread clutched Libby's stomach. She didn't like the way Caleb looked at Elsa. *Is that what he's planning—to see her often?*

Libby didn't like that idea at all. She wished she hadn't brought Elsa to her pa's cabin. Now Caleb would see her whenever they had school.

An empty feeling grew in the pit of Libby's stomach. Sometimes it meant she was going to throw up. Now the feeling came from one thought. *It's all right if Elsa and Caleb are friends. But what if he really likes her?*

❀

During class that afternoon, Caleb leaped up from the table. "We're almost there! Reads Landing, here we come!"

The village lay at the foot of Lake Pepin. Libby and the others followed Caleb to the window. Already they could see paddlewheelers tied up in the open water at Reads Landing. Libby started counting the steamboats.

"There are at least ten!" she exclaimed. "Will we be racing all those boats?"

"Probably more," Caleb told her. "Some are waiting at the town of Wabasha."

Wabasha was the village just below Reads Landing. To Libby's surprise, Caleb didn't seem at all concerned about the odds against them. He just looked forward to the race.

As though held in the palm of a hand, Reads Landing was surrounded on three sides by tall bluffs. On the fourth side lay the river. The minute the gangplank went down, Libby, Caleb, and Elsa left the *Christina*. As they walked along the riverfront, Libby studied each steamboat.

Some came from great distances—as far away as Cincinnati and other places on the Ohio River. Yet nothing could convince Libby that any of them—not even the big, newer boats—were as beautiful as Pa's.

Soon the three of them started up one of the steep streets. From high on the hill they looked across the roofs of houses and hotels to the steamboats and tall smokestacks that Libby loved.

I wish I had my paints along, she thought. If there was time, she would come back by herself.

From an earlier trip, Caleb knew about an overlook upstream and closer to the river. "It might still be a long wait before the ice goes out," he said.

Libby knew it was dangerous trying to get through the ice. Usually the river above and below was free of ice for two weeks before the lake. "How do captains know when it's safe to go through?" she asked.

"They don't always know." Caleb pointed to a narrow line of water between the riverbank and the ice. "When the river starts rising, that open space gets wider. Sometimes boats try to go through, but it's too shallow. If the wind shifts, the ice smashes the boat." Caleb smacked his hands together.

A soft breeze lifted Elsa's white-blond hair. In the crisp air, her pale cheeks had turned rosy with color.

She's beautiful! Once again jealousy stirred within Libby.

As they walked back, she barely saw the large steamboats tied side by side along the riverfront. Like a green-eyed caterpillar, one thought wormed its way into her mind. *I wonder if Caleb is sweet on Elsa.*

❧

When they reached the *Christina*, Libby learned that the famous captain Daniel Smith Harris hadn't arrived. A big part of Libby felt glad. If the four-time winner wasn't part of the race, Pa would have a better chance. Yet Libby knew her father had looked forward to seeing his friend.

The next morning, Libby woke with a start. The *Christina* was moving! Did that mean the race was on?

Quickly Libby dressed and hurried out to the hurricane deck. Far above, the tall stacks belched smoke. On the decks below, passengers crowded the railings, straining for the best view.

With paddle wheels churning the cold, dark water, the *Christina* steamed upriver to the great wide spot called Lake Pepin. "Maybe this is the day the lake will open!" Libby exclaimed when Caleb sat down beside her on the deck.

"I just want your pa to win!" he said. "Think how exciting that would be!"

Libby hardly dared dream about what winning could mean to her father. All summer long the *Christina* went back and forth between St. Louis and St. Paul. If Pa won the race, the *Christina* could dock in St. Paul during the entire season without paying.

As the *Christina* drew near the great mass of ice blocking the river channel, Libby watched closely. In the early morning light, the ice looked gray and soft and spongy. But the ice was stronger than it looked.

Three other daring boats were ahead of them. One was the *War Eagle*, and Libby saw Captain Kingman wave to Pa. Another was the *Galena* with Captain Laughton. His pilot, Stephen Hanks, grinned down at Caleb.

"Is he a friend of yours?" Libby asked.

"Talked to him last night," Caleb said. "He's first cousin to a senator from Illinois. Man by the name of Abraham Lincoln."

Just then the *Christina* slowed her paddles and butted her bow against the ice. The jolt passed through the boat and into Libby. On the deck below, the crowd cheered.

Again and again the *Christina's* pilot stopped, reversed the paddle wheels, pulled back, then started forward again. Again and again the *Christina* butted into the ice. Finally it divided, making a narrow pathway. When the *Christina* steamed into the open water, the crowd raised a shout.

Before long the ice closed again. No amount of pushing against it would break it open. Finally Captain Norstad gave the order to return to Reads Landing. As the *Christina* backed stern first out of the narrow channel, Libby felt the sharp knife of disappointment.

Caleb looked just as discouraged. "Maybe tomorrow," he said.

But Libby knew that the other boats had already gone out every day for a week.

❋

As two days passed into three, passengers on the *Christina* grew impatient. On her way to visit Elsa, Libby saw groups of men talking together on the deck. Mr. Meyer was one of those who asked questions.

"Above Lake Pepin the river is open," said one of the men. "Smaller boats that usually travel on just the Minnesota River come from St. Paul to Red Wing."

"Yah?" Mr. Meyer asked. "And how do we get to Red Wing?"

"There's a trail around Lake Pepin," the man answered. "If we walk to Red Wing, we can book passage to St. Paul. Or we can go wherever we want. We'll beat the other passengers to the best land."

Beat the other passengers, Libby thought as she hurried on. With each passing hour, the men waiting for the ice to go out felt more afraid.

When Libby found Elsa, her friend invited her to sit down in the family's crowded space. "Today I teach you German," Elsa said.

Pretending that she was a teacher, Elsa made her face solemn. "First word. *Auf wiedersehen*." She pronounced it carefully for Libby: "Owf vee-der-zay-en."

"Auf wiedersehen!" Libby could barely say it. "I gave you easy English words! You're giving me something really hard!"

Elsa giggled. "It means 'Until we meet again.' Soon I say goodbye to you. Yah?"

Feeling torn, Libby nodded. Elsa was the best girlfriend she'd had since leaving Chicago. But if Elsa left, maybe Caleb would forget about her.

Libby pushed the thought aside. "I will miss you," she said softly. "Let's not say auf wiedersehen today."

When Mr. Meyer joined his family, a worried frown lined his face. "I need to leave you here," he told Elsa's mother. "I need to find good land—land along the river where there is water for our cattle."

"Yah?" Mrs. Meyer asked. "And there's a way around the ice?"

"A way to walk," Mr. Meyer answered.

"It is dangerous?"

"Yah. It is dangerous, but the only way. I must go now to Red Wing before the best land is gone."

As his wife offered him a cracker, Mr. Meyer shook his head, then glanced toward Libby and Elsa.

"Libby?" Mrs. Meyer asked. "You like a cracker?"

"Thank you, no," Libby answered quickly.

When Elsa took a cracker, she ate it slowly, as if wanting to make every bite last.

So, Libby thought. *The sausage is gone. They're down to crackers now.*

Unable to watch Elsa eat, Libby stood up. *I'll get even more food from Granny.* As she walked away, Libby felt afraid for her friend.

13

Caleb's Warning

The next morning a large group of men and boys left the *Christina*. Mr. Meyer was among them. As Elsa said goodbye to her father, her eyes looked wide and scared.

Captain Norstad stood near the gangplank watching the men go. "I'm sorry," he said again and again.

"Why do you say that, Pa?" Libby asked as the last man walked down the gangplank.

"I know what a hard trip it will be. It's a long, dangerous walk. I wanted to bring them safely into St. Paul." Captain Norstad shook his head. "I've never seen such a late spring! It's hard to believe it's the last week in April!"

Walking to the bow of the *Christina*, he stared upstream. Watching him, Libby remembered Ma and her way of telling Pa that she loved him. Coming to stand beside him, Libby said, "I guess it's time for a wink."

When her father laughed, Libby felt better. "Did you see how those men hated to leave you?" she asked. "You're a good captain, Pa. Those men didn't have any choice."

"I know, Libby," her father answered. "But thanks for re-minding me."

"Caleb said something once—that you've got a good name. What did he mean?"

Pa smiled. "The Norstad name is something to be proud of, Libby."

"I like it because of you," she answered. "But why do you feel that way?"

"For generations the Norstad name has stood for something. For men who are strong and have courage. For men who make good choices, even when it's hard."

"And the women?" Libby asked. "What about the girls? Did they have courage?"

"They've been like you, Libby," her father answered. "I told you about your mother. But don't forget, you're a Norstad too."

Barely breathing, Libby listened. *I'll never have the courage I need*, she thought. Aloud she asked, "What did those Norstad girls know that I don't?"

Her father's smile told Libby that he believed in her. "Every time you make a good choice, even though you're scared, you'll grow a bit. You'll learn what it means to have courage. Some-times it's just doing the next thing."

"Something right in front of you?" Libby asked. Again she wanted more courage. Yet when she thought about all the things that could happen, she felt scared right down to her toes.

❋

That afternoon Samson came for Libby. Standing outside her room, he barked. "Woof!"

When Libby paid no attention, he barked again. "Wooof!"

Libby opened the door. Samson barked so seldom that when he did, she knew he wanted something. As she went out on the deck, Samson moved toward the stairway. When Libby did not follow, he came back to her. With his soft mouth, he took her hand and tugged.

"What do you want, Samson?" Libby asked as she followed him across the deck.

At the steps the big Newfoundland dropped his hold and started down. When he reached the deck below, he waited to be sure that Libby followed. The minute she caught up to him, he started out again. Each time Libby stopped, Samson came back to get her, then went on.

"What's wrong, Samson?" Libby asked when they reached the main deck. By now she felt sure she knew where he was going. More than once, Samson had brought her to Elsa. This time he seemed to have a special urgency.

Soon they reached the Meyer family's small area. The pile of wood was gone, eaten up by the furnaces, and not yet replaced. Elsa lay on the cold deck, the quilts from Libby over her head and body. Only Elsa's face showed.

Mrs. Meyer sat on the deck beside her, crooning something in German and sponging Elsa's face with water. Even on the open deck, the smell of sickness hung in the air.

Moving close to Elsa, Samson stood there as if wanting her to say "Good dog!" When he woofed, Elsa reached out her hand and Samson dropped down on the deck beside her. Elsa's lips curved up in a weak smile. As though weighted, her eyes opened, then closed.

Then beneath the quilt, Elsa's legs twitched. As she pulled up her knees, her eyes flew open. A moan of pain escaped her lips.

Watching her, Libby felt scared. From the time they met, Elsa had seemed too pale, too thin, too fragile. How long had she eaten any kind of food she could get? How long had she gone without being warm? Or having a home?

More than once Pa had talked about the long voyage across the Atlantic. After a crowded trip in which immigrants were exposed to filth and disease, they transferred to a steamboat in New Orleans. With that came still another change in water and food.

Kneeling down next to her friend, Libby spoke to her. "Elsa!"

Suddenly Elsa gasped. As she gagged, Mrs. Meyer reached for a pail.

"I'm going for help," Libby said quickly. As she started away, she remembered Pa had gone into Reads Landing. *Maybe I should find Caleb. He'd know what to do.*

Then a thought leaped into Libby's mind. *Caleb likes Elsa more than me.*

A hot flush rushed into Libby's cheeks. *I can't believe I thought that.* With shame she remembered Pa's talk about the Norstad courage.

For a moment Libby stood there, trying to decide what to do. *Am I going to be jealous of Elsa? Or am I going to take care of her?*

Whirling around, Libby started back to where Elsa lay. By the time Libby reached her friend again, she had a plan. Kneeling down close to Mrs. Meyer, Libby spoke softly so the other deck passengers wouldn't hear. "I want to take Elsa to my room. She'll have a bed and be warmer away from the water."

As gratitude flashed into Mrs. Meyer's eyes, Libby knew that she understood. Quickly Elsa's mother pulled together their few belongings and put them in the trunk.

Libby leaned close to Elsa. "I'm taking you to my room," she whispered. "Do you think you can walk?"

Elsa's eyelids drifted open and she nodded. Then a spasm of pain hit her. Groaning, she clutched the calf of one leg.

When Elsa's cramps passed, Libby lifted one of Elsa's arms and put it over her shoulder. "Stand up," Libby prodded.

Mrs. Meyer slipped under Elsa's other arm. With Elsa between them, Libby and Mrs. Meyer staggered toward the stairs. Taking one step at a time, they climbed to the boiler deck. Half dragging, half carrying Elsa, they continued along that deck.

On the narrower stairway to the hurricane deck it was even more difficult. At last they reached the texas deck and Libby's room. There Elsa fell across the bed. Her mother helped her get settled.

Libby's trunk stood against the door on the far side of the room. Opening the door, Libby pushed it out on the deck. Just then she saw Jordan. "Help me, will you?" Libby asked. She led him down the steps to bring up the Meyer family trunk.

"What happened to Elsa?" Jordan asked when everything was set in place, and they once more stood on the texas deck.

"She's really sick," Libby explained. "She's throwing up, but it isn't flu. Her legs pull up in cramps, and she hurts bad!"

Libby stopped at the look on Jordan's face. Even when some-one as awful as Riggs chased him, Jordan hadn't looked as afraid as he did now.

"You know what Elsa gots?"

Libby shook her head. "Something real bad. Tell Granny, will you, and ask her what to do? And try to find Caleb."

❊

Sitting on the deck with her back against the wall near her room, Libby waited. *If only Pa were here. Or Caleb. Or Granny.*

Libby's tumbled thoughts didn't get anywhere. She wished she knew how to pray the way Pa and Caleb and Jordan did.

As though trying to comfort Libby, Samson flopped down on the deck beside her. Now and then Libby heard Mrs. Meyer speak to Elsa in German. Then Elsa's mother read to her from their big family Bible. Libby didn't understand any of the words.

Each time Elsa groaned, Libby flinched, unable to bear the sound of her friend's pain. Just when Libby felt she could bear the waiting no longer, Jordan returned.

"I can't find either Caleb or Granny," he said. "Maybe they went into Reads Landing with Captain Norstad."

Libby sighed. Standing up, she walked farther down the deck so that Elsa wouldn't hear.

"Jordan, do you think you could find that doctor who came on board in St. Louis? Fenton, I think his name is."

"I ain't got no liking for that man," Jordan answered.

"You don't?" Libby stared at him. "Why not?"

"When I see that man, I gits the jiggles right here." Jordan pointed to the center of his chest.

"The *jiggles*?" Libby asked. "What do you mean? When I talked to him in Keokuk, he seemed like a kind man."

Jordan stiffened. "It ain't what he does, but how he *is*."

An uncomfortable feeling washed over Libby. She didn't want to push aside Jordan's opinion. Somehow he had an unusual way of knowing about people. At the same time, Libby felt desperate.

Lifting her head, she tossed her curls and pushed aside her uneasiness. "Elsa needs a doctor. We only have Doctor Fenton. Please get him."

Jordan's gaze dropped to the floor. With bowed head and slumped shoulders, he turned toward the stairs.

No, wait! Libby wanted to cry out. But her terror for Elsa kept her from speaking.

❋

A short time later, Libby heard footsteps on the stairs and looked down over the railing. Sure enough, Jordan was coming up. He walked quickly, now and then looking back to make sure the doctor followed. When Jordan reached Libby, he did not meet her eyes. Instead, he stood off from her, his head bowed.

By the time Doctor Fenton reached them, he was panting. He set his black doctor's bag down on the deck.

Inside Libby's room Mrs. Meyer sat on a chair next to the bed. When she saw the doctor, she stood up and moved out of the way. Leaving the door open, Doctor Fenton stepped in. Hands behind his back, he stared down over his small, round glasses.

Suddenly Elsa struggled up on one elbow. When she gagged, the doctor jerked back. "She's certainly sick, all right," he said quickly.

Again Elsa gagged. Grabbing a pail, her mother held it beneath Elsa's chin.

In the next instant, the doctor backed out of the room. "Just keep on doing what you're doing," he said, flinging his words at Mrs. Meyer.

Without another look, the doctor hurried past Libby. When he reached the edge of the deck, he turned back and snatched up his bag. Then his feet clattered down the stairs.

When the sound of his footsteps died away, Libby looked at Jordan. Farther along the deck, he still stood with his head bowed. As she walked over to him, Libby's embarrassment felt like a bad taste in her mouth.

"I'm sorry, Jordan," she said. "Sorry I sent you after Doctor Fenton."

"That's all right, Libby."

"For a doctor he sure didn't do much," Libby said.

"That man ain't no doctor."

"I know that now." Libby ached inside. "I wish I had listened to you."

Jordan's troubled gaze met hers. "I knows you is hurtin' for Elsa."

As Libby realized Jordan understood, she began to cry. "I'm afraid Elsa's going to die," she wailed. "And I don't know what to do!"

"Back home—" Jordan stopped as though remembering he no longer had a home. "When we gits sick, we pray."

Again Libby felt humbled. Living with Auntie Vi, she had seen people pray. Their prayers were stiff and formal—solemn words that sounded like people were trying to impress God. How could prayers like that help Elsa?

The few times she herself had prayed, Libby wasn't sure if God had done something or if it had been just a coincidence. Then she remembered how real God seemed to Jordan. Libby decided she'd better be honest. "I don't know how to pray," she said.

"You don't know how?" Jordan asked.

Embarrassed, Libby shook her head. "I hear Pa pray, and I hear you and Caleb pray. But I don't know if God listens to me."

"Prayin' ain't hard," Jordan told her. "Just talk to Jesus like you talk to anyone. But Jesus, He help you a whole lot more."

❈

When Caleb heard about Elsa being sick, he took the stairs to the texas deck two at a time. As soon as he found Libby, he wanted to know all of Elsa's symptoms.

"She's really sick, Caleb. She throws up and gets cramps in her legs and moans with pain."

"And you helped her climb all these steps?" Caleb asked.

When Libby nodded, Caleb's face turned white with dread. Seeing his expression, Libby's insides tied into a knot. *He likes Elsa so much.*

She felt jealous again, but now it was more than a twinge. *I wish Caleb liked me the way he likes Elsa.*

Quickly Libby pushed the thought away. *That's not what counts. What's important is that Elsa gets well.*

"Do you know what she has?" Caleb asked.

Libby shook her head. Seeing Caleb's expression, her fear returned.

"It's cholera!" he said, his voice harsh.

"Kol-er-ah?" Libby whispered. Everyone she knew panicked the minute they heard the word. "You're sure that's what it is?"

"I'm sure." Caleb spit out the words.

At first Libby wondered if he was angry at her. Then she remembered. Caleb's parents had died of cholera.

"Go," he said now. "Wash your hands and your face. And don't go back into that room."

"But Elsa needs my help."

"Her mother will take care of her."

Caleb knocked on the door and waited until Elsa's mother came out. "Elsa must drink and drink and drink." He motioned as though lifting a glass of water to his mouth. "She needs lots of water."

"Yah," Mrs. Meyer said as if she understood.

"I'll bring water to you," Caleb said. "You"—he pointed to Mrs. Meyer—"wash your hands often."

When she nodded, Caleb started toward the captain's cabin. Partway there, he met a steward bringing up a pitcher of water, soap, and a towel.

"Set it down," Caleb told him. He turned back to Mrs. Meyer. "Like this," he said.

There on the deck in front of the staring steward, Caleb

washed his face and hands and arms.

"You, too, Libby," he said. "Don't forget. It's your life, you know."

His words were solemn—so solemn that Libby wanted to say, "Nothing will happen to me!"

Then she saw Caleb's eyes. In spite of his strong words, he was too scared to listen to any of her proud remarks.

14

I'll Show Them!

"*D*on't think you're stronger than everyone else," Caleb warned. "That you're the only one who won't get sick!"

It was as though Caleb had read her mind, and Libby didn't like the feeling. "How did you know?" she asked.

"Because that's how I felt once." Caleb turned toward Captain Norstad's cabin.

Libby started down the stairs to the boiler deck. The women's washroom was just behind the paddle wheel on the starboard, or right, side of the boat when looking toward the bow. She would go there and wash her face and hands, the way Caleb said.

As though unwilling to leave her, Samson followed close behind. Outside the washroom, the large dog dropped down on his haunches. When Libby came back out, he was sniffing at something hairy. "Oh, ick!" Libby told him. "Have you got a dead mouse?"

Samson paid no attention. Instead, he flipped his head, tossing whatever it was in the air. When it fell to the deck, the dog again pushed it with his nose.

Sure now that it wasn't a mouse, Libby felt curious. "Here, Samson," she said. "What have you got?"

Raising his head, Samson looked at Libby. On the deck lay a big handlebar mustache. Suddenly Libby grasped the awfulness of what she was seeing. "Oh no!"

Kneeling down, she picked up the mustache by the stiff curl at one end. Touching it no more than she had to, Libby stared at it. Without doubt it was the one she had seen on the man who looked like Riggs!

Holding the mustache at arm's length, Libby headed for the stairs. *I need to tell Caleb and Pa!*

Samson followed close behind. On the way to the captain's cabin, Libby almost crashed into Jordan. "Take a look at this!" she exclaimed. "Riggs lost his mustache, and Samson found it!"

Libby started to tremble. "It's just like we thought. Riggs really *is* on board! Why hasn't he grabbed you?"

"He takin' his time, Libby."

"What do you mean?"

"He knows how strong I is." Jordan flexed his muscle and grinned. Then his eyes grew solemn. "When Riggs knows everything he wants to know, he'll just git some catchers to help. Then he tuck this boy under his arm and carry him off."

Libby stared at Jordan. "C'mon. We've got to tell Pa."

When she reached her father's cabin, Libby flung open the door. Caleb sat at the table, talking with Pa. Jordan and Samson followed Libby inside.

"Riggs is here!" she announced.

"On board?" her father asked. "How do you know?"

"Look what Samson found!" Libby dropped the mustache onto the table.

Her father looked puzzled. "You'd better explain what's going on."

"Caleb and I wondered if Riggs came on board in St. Louis," Libby said. "As I stood near the gangplank, I saw a man dressed like Riggs. He carried a cane with a gold handle."

"There's more than one wealthy man who carries a gold-headed cane," Pa answered, as though not wanting to believe Riggs was on board. "And sometimes a cane like that is given to honor someone."

"But it was more, Pa," Libby said. "The man I saw was short and slender and even walked like Riggs. The one thing that was different was his big handlebar mustache. At first I thought, 'That can't be him. Riggs couldn't grow a mustache in one day.' Then I decided it might be his disguise."

"Do you know whether this man really did come on board?" Pa asked.

"We weren't sure at first," Libby answered. "Then Jordan wondered if he saw Riggs, and I saw the man in the dining room. I was going to follow him and find out which stateroom was his. But I lost him."

"Where did Samson find the mustache?" Pa asked.

"On the boiler deck. Where the first-class passengers walk around for exercise."

"And you, Caleb?" asked the captain. "Have you seen this man?"

Caleb shook his head. "When Libby told me about him, I checked the passenger lists. If Riggs *is* on board, he didn't use his own name. But Libby probably is right. She has a good memory for faces."

"What about you, Jordan?" the captain asked. "What do you think about all this?"

"That man Riggs is like a cat ready to pounce. I is feeling more and more like a mouse. But I can't let Riggs catch me because I gots to get my family free."

Captain Norstad stood up and strolled over to the window. Libby knew it was his thinking-things-through walk. More than once she had seen it when a decision needed to be made. Caleb seemed to recognize the same thing, for he, too, waited quietly, not speaking.

At the window Captain Norstad looked down. Libby's gaze followed his. Far below, the sparkling waters of the Mississippi flowed past the *Christina*. Libby wished that all their problems could fall behind the same way.

Turning back to them, her father spoke. "We have cholera on board." His voice was rough, as if trying to push aside his concern. "We have Riggs on board. We have Jordan on board."

"I'll git off the boat," Jordan said quickly. "If Riggs can't find me, he can't blame you for hiding me."

The captain straightened his shoulders. "Maybe we can take care of all three problems with one quick move."

Libby glanced over to where a chessboard sat on a small table near the wall. *But this isn't a game*, she thought as she looked back to her father.

"Caleb, tomorrow morning before first light, you and Jordan leave the *Christina*. Follow the Indian trails around Lake Pepin. It's a long, cold walk, but there's a doctor in Red Wing—a man named William Sweney. Four years ago, a steamboat came to Red Wing with seventeen cholera patients on board. Doctor Sweney put them in a building near the Old Spring Creek Mill. Every day he visited them."

Libby's thoughts flew to Elsa. "What happened?" Libby asked.

"Out of seventeen patients, ten lived," her father told her.

Suddenly Libby dared to hope. "If Elsa could be like the ten—"

"We'll hope, and we'll pray," Pa said.

Libby glanced toward Caleb. He looked relieved, as though he, too, now hoped that Elsa might get well.

"When people hear the word *cholera*, everyone panics," Captain Norstad said. "But when Doctor Sweney took care of those patients, not one person in the town of Red Wing got sick."

The captain looked first at Caleb, then at Jordan. "Find Doctor Sweney. If he'll come, bring him to us. If Lake Pepin doesn't open soon, we could have an epidemic on our hands."

An epidemic? Libby knew that like wildfire, a disease could spread from one person to another.

"We'll do our best," Caleb promised.

"While you're gone, I'll tell the deck passengers to take their belongings onto land," the captain answered. "We'll scrub down the areas where they've been living and sleeping. Maybe that will keep them from getting sick."

The fear was gone now in Caleb's eyes, replaced by respect. "I've never known a captain to do that."

"I have," Libby's father answered. "The captain who did it stopped an epidemic."

"What if the ice goes out while you're cleaning up?" Caleb asked. "You'll miss the race to St. Paul."

"It's a risk we have to take." Captain Norstad sounded as if he had already thought about that. "If we don't, we can be sure that many of the deckers will lose their lives."

The captain turned to Jordan. "Get warm clothes from Caleb. Under the tall pines there will still be slush and ice where the sun doesn't reach. If all goes well, you'll reach Red Wing by four or five o'clock."

If all goes well, Libby thought as Caleb started for the door.

"Just a minute," Captain Norstad said.

Caleb turned back. "Sir?"

"Take Libby with you."

"Libby?" Caleb's protest sounded like a groan. "I have to take *her*?"

"That's what I asked."

As Caleb glanced toward Libby, she stiffened. More than anything, she wanted to go, to bring back help for Elsa. Yet it was clear that Caleb didn't want her along.

"Libby, take a small bundle of extra clothes in case you get wet," Pa said. "But don't carry more than you need."

The warm feeling that Pa believed in her welled up inside of Libby. He knew she could do something hard and succeed. "I'll do my best, Pa," Libby promised.

"I know you will." His long look matched hers.

"I need to move into your cabin." As Libby explained about helping Elsa to her room, she caught Pa's quick glance toward

Caleb. Was Pa wondering if she had already caught cholera from Elsa?

When Libby went out, she left the door open just a crack. Stepping to one side, she leaned against the wall and listened.

"Sir." Caleb's voice was courteous.

Always Libby felt surprised at the relationship between Caleb and her father. More than any other person, Caleb felt free to say what he liked to Pa. Often Captain Norstad talked with him about his decisions, as though to help Caleb understand his reasons. And once Pa had said, "I would trust Caleb even with my life."

"I want you to take Libby," the captain said now, as though knowing what Caleb was going to say.

"She'll slow us down. She'll be nothing but trouble."

Libby strained to hear, but her father did not answer.

"There will be mud and bears and snakes." Caleb paused as though thinking of more reasons why Libby shouldn't go along.

"And ice and sharp limestone and danger," the captain answered.

"Sir." Caleb's voice was quieter now, as though he were thinking it through. "You want her off the *Christina*, don't you? You're afraid that if Libby stays, she'll get cholera. Do you know how much she's already been around Elsa?"

Again Libby strained to hear. When her father did not answer, Libby knew. *It isn't that he thinks I'm brave. If there's an epidemic, he wants me far away.*

Suddenly the warm feelings inside Libby vanished. With it went her hope that her father believed in her.

All that big talk about knowing I'll do my best! Anger raced through Libby, leaving a bitter taste. *We're a never-give-up family, all right!*

When Pa did not answer Caleb, Libby knew the matter was decided in spite of Caleb's protest.

Then Libby heard Caleb's steps coming toward her. In a flash she leaped away from the door. As Caleb left the cabin, she raced toward her room.

I'll show them! Libby promised herself. *I'll show both Pa and Caleb that I can do more than they think!*

15

Red Is for Courage

"*You're not the kind of girl to live in this wilderness!*" As Libby decided what clothes she'd take, Caleb's words spun around in her head.

Soon after she met him, Caleb had let her know what he thought of her fancy dresses. According to him, women coming into this newly settled area should be proud to wear a jean dress or a checked apron.

Well, I'll surprise you, Caleb Whitney! In secret she had sewn a skirt made from jean cloth. Now it was ready to wear.

Then Libby remembered her hair. Caleb hadn't liked her long, red curls either. They were combed out now, and her hair pulled back. Yet Libby was certain that in no time her hair would be full of twigs.

When ready for the next day, Libby spread the quilts she hadn't given Elsa on the floor of Pa's cabin. Still feeling upset with both Pa and Caleb, she fell asleep.

Hours later Libby had a nightmare. In her dream she knew she had to rescue Pa. Over and over she called for help, but her voice wouldn't come.

As she tried to cry out, Pa shook her awake. "Libby! Wake up!"

At first she didn't understand what was happening. Then she began to sob.

"What's wrong, Libby?" Pa asked as she came awake. "Are you afraid of the walk to Red Wing?"

Libby shook her head. "I dreamed that something was happening to you."

"Something bad?"

Between sobs, she nodded.

"Oh, Libby!" Pa exclaimed.

She heard him moving about, then saw a soft glow as he lit the lamp next to his rocking chair. Pa led Libby over to the chair, sat down, and pulled her onto his lap.

Not since she was a little girl had Pa rocked her, and Libby felt almost silly. She was really too big to fit on his lap, but Pa's arms went around her.

For a time he rocked her, saying little. Then he asked, "Libby, do you worry about what might happen to me?"

Her face tucked against his chest, she nodded. Then she remembered Pa's talk with Caleb. "Do you worry about what might happen to *me*?" she asked.

"I try not to," Pa answered. "But I want to be careful, to be wise about taking care of you."

"Is that why you're sending me with Caleb?"

"It's a hard choice, Libby. It seems to be the lesser of two evils."

"So you don't really think I'm strong and courageous." Libby began crying again. "The worst of it is, I'm *not*!" she wailed. Her nightmare still seemed real. "I get so scared about *you*!"

When her sobs quieted, Pa spoke gently. "Libby, I'm your Pa. It's my job to take care of you, but it's not your job to take care of me. No matter how hard you try, you won't be able to do it."

"Then what do I do?"

"Maybe you'd better let God take care of me."

God. There it is again, Libby thought. "Are you sure God can manage?" she asked.

Pa smiled. "I'm sure," he said. "Even if the very worst happened, God would be with me. He's the one who takes care of both of us. Wherever we are, He *is*."

Reaching out, Pa pulled the lamp closer to them. "Do you see this, Libby?" he asked.

She nodded. More than once she had noticed the lamp. Inside the glass base, a piece of red flannel floated in the oil.

"This lamp always reminds me of your ma," Pa said. "Christina was like a lot of pioneer women. She put the flannel in the lamp to remind herself that red is for courage."

"You've told me that before—that Ma had courage." Yet it seemed as though everything Libby tried had worked out wrong. "How did Ma get courage?"

Pa rested a hand on his big Bible. "Your mother found verses—promises that helped her trust the Lord. There's one she liked especially much. 'Fear thou not, for I am with thee; be not dismayed; for I am thy God.'"

Startled, Libby sat up. *The words I heard down in the hold! So that's how I knew them!* Libby's voice joined Pa's. "'I will strengthen thee; yea, I will help thee.'"

Strangely comforted, she looked Pa in the eyes. "Did Ma teach me that verse?"

Pa smiled. "I wouldn't be surprised. Whenever she needed courage, she repeated those words over and over again."

❁

When it was time to leave, Pa looked Libby straight in the eye. "Don't forget you're a Norstad, Libby. And remember your mother's verse."

Pa's hug felt warm and strong, making Libby believe she really could walk all those miles to Red Wing. *Maybe Elsa will get well, after all. If only we can find Doctor Sweney and bring him back in time.*

It was still dark when Caleb led Libby and Jordan down the

gangplank. Without making a sound, they crept up the steep bank next to the river. The town was quiet now. Even the nearby steamboats lay silent.

Then Libby heard footsteps from behind. She strained to listen. There it was again—the sound of boots on the gangplank.

Libby tugged at Caleb's arm. She barely heard his warning shush, but she knew. Caleb had also heard the footsteps.

When he picked up his pace, Libby and Jordan stayed with him. As they passed one of the town's seventeen hotels, a dog started barking. Caleb walked even faster. They were a short distance beyond the hotel when the dog fell quiet.

Moments later he barked again, and Caleb hurried on. As silence filled the darkness before dawn, Libby once more heard footsteps. Soon Caleb slipped into the shadows between large warehouses. Libby and Jordan joined him in the darkness.

In a few minutes, three dark shapes hurried past them. As Libby caught her breath, Caleb's warning fingers tightened on her arm.

Along the streets of Reads Landing, no one else stirred. Before long, the footsteps of the three men died away. Caleb slipped out from between the buildings. For a short distance, he walked along the street next to the river. Nearby, the great steamboats rose from the water. In the darkness their tall stacks seemed to disappear.

At a street leading upward, Caleb turned. On the hillside above the waterfront, he turned again, this time onto a dirt street that ran the same direction as the river. Near the north end of town, the street became a road. Muddy now from wagons bringing wheat and other goods to Reads Landing, the road looked well used.

Caleb set a rapid pace, walking around the holes and puddles whenever possible. Then suddenly he left the road. When he came to a small shed, he crouched down behind it.

Kneeling between Caleb and Jordan, Libby listened. It wasn't long before she heard the sound of men walking toward Reads Landing. One of them was angry.

"What happened?" he asked. "We were just behind them."

"We can't let that slave boy get away!" growled another.

As soon as the men were safely past, Caleb returned to the road. They had walked some distance before Libby dared speak.

"Have you gone this way before?"

"Nope," Caleb answered.

"How do you know where you're going?"

"Your pa told me. Other men described it to him. Soon we'll follow an old Indian trail."

"One they've walked for years and years?"

Caleb nodded. "And before them, the buffalo. Indians followed their trails because buffalo find the easiest way. That's what we'll try to do."

"How far is it to Red Wing?" Libby asked.

"By river, twenty-eight miles. Your pa isn't sure how far it is by land."

Twenty-eight miles? Libby gulped, then tried to hide her feelings from Caleb. *Pa thinks I can walk twenty-eight miles? Maybe he believes in me more than I think.*

For the first time, Libby felt really shaky about the trip. She tried to remember if she'd ever done anything to prepare for this. In Chicago she had sometimes walked long distances, but never anything like twenty-eight miles.

"When we get to Wacouta, we might find someone to take us the rest of the way," Caleb said. "There are supposed to be hotels and a trading post there."

"And how far is Wacouta?" Libby asked.

"Five or six miles from Red Wing," Caleb answered, as if he walked such distances every day. And probably he did, more often than Libby liked to think.

"What if we can't reach Red Wing tonight?" she asked.

Caleb shrugged. "Your pa said there might be a cave in the bluffs."

Across Libby's back she carried a cloth bag holding extra clothes. A smaller bag tied around her waist held sandwiches and cookies packed by Granny. Like Libby, the boys had tied their bags on their back or waist to keep their hands free. Caleb had extra gear, including a bucket that hung from a rope around his waist.

Walking behind him, Libby noticed the set of his shoulders. She could almost hear him say, "Your pa said I had to take you along, but I don't like it."

Well, I don't like the way you feel! Libby wanted to tell him. *Elsa is my friend too. I want to help her!*

Close behind, Jordan walked without saying a word. More than once Libby turned to look back and saw Jordan glancing over his shoulder. It frightened her.

When the slave catchers don't find us, will they turn around again? Libby wondered. The mud on the road would make it easy for them to follow. *Maybe they're tracking us even now. Maybe they're just far enough back so we can't see.*

A few miles above Reads Landing, Caleb brought them to a high stretch of ground overlooking Lake Pepin. As the sky turned gold and pink, the sun lit the great expanse of ice. People had told Libby that at places the lake was three miles wide, but she never expected anything so beautiful. In spite of her worries, she wanted to take in everything and remember it all. *Someday I'll paint this!* she promised herself.

As they hurried on, tall bluffs rose above them on their left. On their right the ground dropped sharply away to the lake. Gradually the road narrowed, then turned into a limestone trail.

By the time Caleb found a large log and sat down, Libby felt hollow with hunger. Even while eating breakfast, Caleb faced back toward the trail over which they had come. Grateful for the chance to rest, Libby dropped down next to him. But Jordan grasped the lower branches of a tall white pine and pulled himself up. From far overhead he, too, checked the trail.

Watching the boys, Libby felt uneasy. Did they still fear Riggs even after miles of fast walking? *It must be hard for Jordon*, Libby thought. *He's helping Elsa when he really wants to get his family to freedom.*

Finally, Jordan climbed down and began to eat. When all of

them finished, Caleb brushed aside his crumbs and Libby did the same.

Using a small pine branch, Jordan swept the ground until their footsteps disappeared. When they returned to the path, he carried the branch along. More than once, dirt had washed over the limestone trail. Where needed, Jordan brushed away their footprints.

As the sun climbed higher, the trail leveled out, and Libby felt grateful. They walked close to the lake now. The sunlight turned the ice into a shining jewel.

Beyond a long point reaching out into Lake Pepin, the ground once again dropped sharply away. Soon after the trail led them farther from the lake, Caleb pointed down to a large paw print. "That's a big one!"

"A big what?" Libby asked, not sure she wanted to know.

"A bear, probably a male. They're hungry now. When they come out of hibernation, they eat everything in sight."

"Food, you mean?" Libby tried to keep the scared sound out of her voice.

"Of course they eat food." A sparkle of fun shot through Caleb's eyes. Then he grew serious. "And little girls."

"Oh, Caleb!" Libby didn't believe him.

"They're especially fond of big girls, whether they're tasty or not."

"You're just making that up!"

But Caleb's face was as serious as she had ever seen it. "If you see a bear—"

"I don't believe a word you're saying!"

"Just stay as far from it as you can. Don't ever get between a female and her cubs!"

Well, that sounds reasonable, Libby thought. *So, is the rest of what he's saying true or not?* When Caleb teased her, she didn't know what to believe.

Libby tossed her head, and her red curls swung around her shoulders. *I refuse to think about it. We'll reach Red Wing before dark—*

by four or five o'clock, Pa said. That will keep me safe from any bears!

Besides, it was Riggs and his two slave catchers that Libby worried about. *They're much more dangerous than any four-footed animal!*

16

Slave Catchers!

*W*hen Caleb would have stopped for a rest, Jordan said no. "What's wrong?" Caleb asked, his voice low.

Jordan looked over his shoulder. "Someone's watching my back."

"What do you mean?" Libby asked.

"Someone's behind us," Jordan answered. "Someone comin' mighty close."

"You didn't see anyone, did you?" Libby asked. "How do you know?"

"I just knows," Jordan told her. "The Lord, He make me uneasy. He say, 'Jordan, you watch your back, or you is goin' to be in big trouble.'"

"Did the Lord tell you what to do?" Caleb asked.

"Leave the path," Jordan said, as though there were no doubt in his mind.

Listening to the boys talk, Libby felt surprised. It was Jordan leading them now, and Caleb seemed to trust Jordan's leading. Stepping aside, Caleb let him take first place. Libby still walked in the middle, but now Caleb followed her.

Jordan stayed off the path, but walked not far from it. When they dropped onto lower ground, they found pockets of snow in the hollows beneath tall white pine. Sheltered from the sun, the snow sometimes lay a foot deep. As it melted, water streamed downhill.

"It's hard to remember it's the last week in April!" Libby exclaimed.

"Don't forget it was one of the worst winters Minnesota Territory has had," Caleb reminded her.

Trudging across land he had never seen, Jordan led them on. Watching him, Libby wondered about other times when he needed to find his own path. Always Jordan walked with a confidence she never seemed to feel.

Though used to a warmer climate, he hiked without seeming tired. After a time he took off the boots Caleb had given him. Tying the laces, he slung the boots over his shoulders, as if more comfortable going barefoot.

Once Libby heard Jordan singing softly, almost under his breath.

I got shoes,
You got shoes,
All God's children got shoes.
When we get to Heaven
We goin' to put on our shoes
An' shout all over God's Heaven.
Heaven! Heaven!

When Caleb and Jordan finally stopped for lunch, Libby was so hungry she could hardly walk another step. Using a large stump as a table, she untied the cloth bag holding her food. For each sandwich, Granny had put together two big pieces of thickly sliced bread with chicken or beef between.

Libby had gobbled up one sandwich and started another when she looked around. *Where did the boys go?* Up till now they hadn't left her alone. Libby didn't like the idea at all.

Just then she heard a branch crack. Her heart leaped. *Caleb?*

Jordan? Are they coming back? They would never make so much noise.

Whirling around, Libby gazed in the direction from which the noise came. When she heard a second cracking sound her stomach bottomed out. *Riggs and his slave catchers! And I'm here alone!*

Forgetting her lunch, Libby stumbled away from the large stump. When she reached a tall tree, she slipped behind the trunk.

On the other side of the clearing, bushes were starting to leaf out. Something black seemed to move behind them. Peering out from behind the tree trunk, Libby watched. Closer and closer, the black shape moved, lumbering along. With every step the shape grew larger.

Suddenly, Libby felt her knees go weak. Without warning she slid to the ground. By the time she felt strong enough to look again, the black creature was out in the open. A great big bear!

Libby had never seen a bear before, but it was so big it had to be a male. On all fours he walked, swaying from side to side. In the sunlight his black hair shone. When he sniffed his way around the clearing, Libby guessed what he wanted.

"You're not getting it!" she muttered.

Leaping up, Libby headed straight for the large stump. With one hand she snatched up her sandwich. With the other, she grabbed the bag with the rest of her food. Then she heard a snuffle, not far away.

Turning, Libby faced the bear. In the next instant he stood up on his hind legs.

"Caleb!" Libby tried to scream. But panic closed her throat.

"Jordan!" she tried again. Not a sound came from her mouth.

With his great brown eyes, the bear sized up Libby. As though spotting the sandwich in her hand, he dropped down and headed straight for her. His mouth opened, showing his great teeth.

"Libby!"

As though from far away, she heard Caleb's voice.

"Drop your sandwich!"

With one quick movement, Libby threw the sandwich from her. Instead of following it, the bear turned toward the cloth bag and sandwiches in her other hand.

"Get rid of your food!" Caleb called.

Libby threw the bag after the sandwich. In that moment the bear turned from her. With a single gulp, he swallowed the sandwich she had thrown.

Unable to run, Libby stared at him. With another great paw, the bear pushed at the cloth bag and sniffed the sandwiches inside.

Just then a hand reached out to grab Libby's arm. As the bear gulped a second sandwich, the hand pulled Libby back.

In terror she tripped, then caught herself. Looking up, she saw Caleb's frightened face.

"Hurry!" he commanded.

Pulling her along, he walked as quickly as she could follow. When they reached the path, Caleb kept going. Faster and faster he moved, with Libby stumbling behind. Only his strong hand kept her from falling in the snowy slush.

After a time Caleb drew her off the path into the trees. When at last he stopped, Libby's side ached from hurrying. Only then did she realize that Jordan was just behind them.

Caleb dropped her hand. Anger filled his face. "I have never in my life—"

"I'm sorry," Libby said quickly.

"You are *sorry* for trying to get killed?"

"I didn't know."

"How can you be so stupid as to take on a bear for one little sandwich?"

Suddenly Libby began to cry. "It was all the food I had," she wailed.

"No, it wasn't." The anger disappeared from Caleb's face. "You had my food and Jordan's food."

Libby giggled. "You're right. I wasn't very smart, was I?" As though it were the funniest thing she'd ever done, she started laughing.

Moments later, tears ran down her cheeks. Her entire body shook with sobs.

"Libby!" Caleb commanded. "Stop it!"

But Libby could not stop crying.

"Libby Norstad!" Caleb's voice filled with panic. Bending down, he scooped up a handful of snow and clapped it across her face.

In that instant both tears and laughter left Libby. Only anger remained.

"You . . . you!" she sputtered. "Who do you think you are?"

Caleb looked relieved. "Your pa said I had to take care of you."

"Well, you have a strange way of doing it!"

"Yup." Caleb seemed pleased with himself now. "When you start going into hysterics, I better do something."

Feeling as if she were going to explode, Libby stared at him. "How can you be so awful?"

Caleb grinned at Jordan. "Guess she's back to normal."

But Libby didn't feel grateful to Caleb. *Why does this terrible boy always have to be right?* she wondered. *I wish that just once he'd make a fool of himself!*

By now she even felt angry with Caleb for rescuing her. With the bear far behind and her fear gone, she wondered about only one thing. *How can I ever win?*

She almost felt like praying. *Just once, God, let me beat Caleb at something.*

Then she pushed the thought aside. From what she knew about God, Libby didn't think He'd answer that prayer.

As though making sure she was all right, Caleb gave her one last look, then started walking again. When he came to some large rocks near Lake Pepin, he stopped.

"Watch out for snakes," he told Libby.

"Snakes!" she exclaimed. That would be even worse than a bear! What other horrors hid out in this wilderness?

Libby turned to Jordan. "Is Caleb teasing?"

Jordan's gaze met hers. "Snakes likes to lie on warm rocks," he said simply.

Libby shuddered, then was sorry she had shown her fear. Opening the cloth bag he carried around his waist, Caleb spread out his lunch. "Help yourself," he told Libby.

But Libby's pride was wounded now. Not for anything was she going to eat Caleb's food. "I'm not hungry," she said.

"Yes, you are," he answered. "You're just proud."

His words upset Libby even more. How could he possibly know how she felt? *Not for anything will I give in now!*

As Libby drew back, her stomach gurgled.

"Hear that rumble?" Caleb asked Jordan without looking at Libby. "How can such a skinny girl need so much food?"

Jordan grinned. "Bet your granny bakes those lip-smackin' pies just for Libby."

"I ate a big breakfast," Libby said, surprised that Jordan dared tease her. Bravely, she backed away. "Thanks anyway."

She looked at the rocks, then remembered what Jordan said about snakes. Walking off a short distance, she sat down on a log. When Caleb chomped down on his sandwich, she glanced away, trying to not think about food.

Along the shore a narrow band of black water separated her from the great mass of ice in Lake Pepin. Although the day was growing warmer all the time, the ice still looked solid.

Before long, Caleb and Jordan closed up their sandwiches.

"I'll figure out which way to go and be right back," Caleb said.

As soon as he disappeared, Jordan offered Libby a sandwich. "I saved it for you," he said. "Eat up now."

Glancing around, Libby saw that the trees hid her from Caleb. Grateful that Jordan had waited until Caleb was gone, Libby took the sandwich.

"Thanks, Jordan," she said.

With her gaze on the trees where Caleb disappeared, Libby wolfed down the sandwich. Quickly she brushed her skirt, making sure that no crumb showed. No sooner had she wiped a hand across her mouth than Caleb returned.

"Let's stay off the path and climb higher," he said.

With Lake Pepin on their right, they headed into the trees. Jordan led again, and Libby fell into line with Caleb behind her. Though they didn't follow the path, they stayed close enough to catch a glimpse now and then. Jordan and Caleb seemed to move in agreement, as if knowing exactly what they were doing.

Soon they started up a steep slope that rose far above the pebbly shores of Lake Pepin. As Libby hiked along, she heard a low voice at her back.

"Take it," Caleb said and pushed a sandwich into her hand.

Libby looked down. With every part of her being, she wanted to grab the sandwich. In spite of what Jordan had given her, she was still hungry. But Libby shook her head.

"We still have a long way to go," Caleb told her. "If you're hungry you'll be weak."

Again Libby hesitated, her pride in the way.

"Elsa needs your help," Caleb said.

Libby's pride vanished. Caleb had given her the one reason she couldn't argue. "Thanks," she said softly.

"Don't mention it."

Libby grinned. "I won't."

Without slowing her pace, she gulped down the sandwich. Granny's chicken and bread had never tasted so good.

For at least fifteen minutes, they walked with the ground growing ever steeper beneath them. More than once Libby clutched at small trees and branches to pull herself up. Finally Jordan stopped.

Behind a thick growth of bushes he waited. When Caleb came close, Jordan pointed to a spot just below them. "There's the path," he said. Both boys crouched low.

Kneeling beside them, Libby stared down the steep hillside. Shrubs hid the path, and Libby wondered how Jordan knew it was there. As the minutes stretched long, she grew impatient.

When she started to speak, Caleb laid a warning hand on her arm. "Shush!"

Moments later Libby heard men's voices. Trying to push aside her nervousness, she listened.

Then just below them, a young man stopped. Through a small opening between bushes, Libby saw his face and blond hair.

I know him! Libby gasped. *He's one of the bullies who chased Jordan! So he's a slave catcher now!*

Squeezing Libby's arm, Caleb warned her to be quiet. Instead, she hiccuped loudly.

As Caleb glared at her, Libby clapped a hand over her mouth. *Oh no! What should I do?*

From somewhere beyond the blond slave catcher came a call. "Hey! What's keeping you?"

Just then Libby felt another hiccup coming. Filled with panic, she tried to hold it in. When she breathed deeply, Caleb clapped his hand over hers. Swallowing hard, Libby gasped.

Suddenly Caleb clutched the back of her head and pushed her face into the ground. When the hiccup came, it was gigantic.

On her head Caleb's fingers stiffened. Desperately Libby held her breath.

Just below them, still another man was talking. His voice seemed familiar to Libby. With a quick flash of fear, she wondered if it was Riggs. Still afraid to breathe, she dreaded the next hiccup. When it came, it seemed to rumble across the hillsides.

At last the three slave catchers passed beyond them. For long minutes Libby and Caleb and Jordan waited, silent and watchful. Then Caleb pounded his fist into the ground. "Libby, I cannot believe how you do it!"

In the next moment, he looked at her and started to laugh. "How can you manage to get hiccups at a time like this?"

Her eyes wide, Libby stared at him. Not for anything in the world would she admit that she had eaten three of Granny's big sandwiches.

17

Danger Signal

"*How* did you know they were still following us?" Libby asked Jordan as they walked on.

"I gots the jiggles right here." He pointed to his heart.

"Jiggles?" Libby asked. "You felt uneasy?"

Jordan nodded. "When I just a little boy, my momma tell me, 'Jordan, when you is doing something that should be good and the Lord wants your attention, you notice the jiggles. You pray, 'What's botherin' me, Lord? Is it you?' If the Lord says, 'Yes'm!' you pay attention."

Libby stared at Jordan. "So it's *God* talking to you? That's really strange!"

Jordan moved quickly now, still being quiet, but not as careful about noise. Slipping and sliding on old wet leaves, they dropped down to a lower part of the bluff.

When Jordan stopped for a minute, Libby wanted to know more. "You still haven't told me how you knew the men were behind us."

"I just hear God say, 'Jordan, hold up now.' "

"In words like that? He spoke out loud?"

"Not this time," Jordan said, as if he had no doubt that God could. "This time He keep it secret like, kind of deep inside."

"No voice?" Libby asked. "But what? How did you know?"

"I just knew."

When Libby threw up her hands, Caleb grinned.

As Jordan started on again, Libby spoke quickly. "No, wait. It's important. How can I hear God the way you do?"

Jordan's smile spread across his face. "You gots to let Jesus git you, Libby. Then you hear Him talk."

❀

The afternoon sun warmed Libby now, and she changed her heavy sweater for a lighter shawl. Though they followed a valley with an easy slope, her legs and feet ached with every step.

"Keep going," Caleb encouraged her. "According to your pa, we'll soon come to Wacouta."

When they reached the edge of town, Libby saw two hotels built on the heights above Lake Pepin. Instead of walking straight into the settlement, Caleb stayed within a line of trees.

"Bullard's Trading Post is at the head of a creek," he told them. "The creek empties into mud flats next to the river."

Beyond the hotels, Caleb led them to a place overlooking the mud flats. On the low ground was a trading post that had to be Bullard's.

"Wait here while I check things out," Caleb said. "If we need a danger signal, call like a crow."

Starting down hill, Caleb ran from tree to tree using branches for protection. As Libby looked beyond Caleb to the trading post, a tall blond fellow stepped around a corner.

"That's the bully who chased you!" Libby told Jordan.

Moments later a brown-haired fellow followed the first. "He chased you too!" Libby exclaimed. "They're both from the *Christina*."

"And they both be slave catchers now," Jordan answered. "But Caleb can't see what we're seein'. He is headin' into a trap."

Crouching down to hide himself, Jordan called out. "*Caw, caw,*

caw!" The sound was so real that Libby could hardly believe it wasn't a crow.

Again Jordan called. *"Caw, caw, caw!"*

From farther away in the woods, a crow answered. *Caw, caw, caw!*

Jordan grinned and called back. This time an owl responded.

Libby stared into the trees, trying to spot the owl. Not far beyond them, it perched high in a tree. As though staking out its territory, it warned away invaders.

When Caleb returned, he had been running. As soon as he caught his breath, they started walking again.

Caleb led them toward a bluff. "Your pa said it's too hard to cross on the wet flats. We'll have to try the bluff."

Climbing higher, they searched for a way across. Before long, they came to a ravine—a deep, narrow valley between steep hills. Cut into limestone or sandstone, the ravine was made of jagged, steplike rocks. Where normally there would be no water, melting snow filled the ravine to overflowing. Swirling through narrow openings, water swept over the ledges.

A tree had fallen across the rushing stream, and Caleb and Jordan used the trunk as a bridge. When Libby followed, she looked down and felt afraid. Though Pa had taught her to swim, she could only think about the rocks below and the coldness of the water.

By the time Caleb stopped next to another runoff ravine, Libby was panting with her effort to keep up. Sinking down beside Caleb, she drew deep breaths. Jordan became the lookout, searching the area below them.

For Libby the trip was starting to feel endless. "Are we ever going to reach Doctor Sweney?" she asked. "Elsa needs help *now.*"

"We're doing pretty well," Caleb encouraged her. "Once we get past this stretch, we'll make better time."

Libby sighed. Taking off her shoes, she rubbed her sore feet. Nearby, ice edged the limestone banks of the stream. In the shadow of the great bluff above them, more ice held back great pools of water.

Caleb pointed to a wedge of ice that lay across the ravine. "Let's hope we're not under one of those if it lets go."

Libby gazed up at the ice dam, then pulled her shoes back on. When they started out again, they used another fallen tree to cross the stream. As Libby followed the boys, the trunk trembled. Again she stared down at the rocks and rushing water. Afraid to go on, she dropped to her hands and knees.

"Hurry up!" Caleb called as she started to crawl.

Instead, Libby inched forward. Finally she jumped onto solid ground.

Minutes later they came to the biggest ravine yet. With this stream there seemed no easy way to cross. At the same time, the ravine was less filled with water than most.

Caleb scouted around, trying to find a way. "The stream empties into a creek," he said when he came back. "It's probably the creek that goes past Bullard's. We don't have any choice but to cross here."

"Maybe there are stepping-stones across the stream." Libby felt relieved that she didn't have to use another fallen tree.

Just then Caleb noticed a ledge in the bluff above them. "I'm going up to see how we're doing," he told Libby and Jordan.

Careful not to set off a shower of rolling stones, Caleb started up the hill. Along the stream, Libby and Jordan kept searching for a place to cross. As they climbed higher, close to the steep wall of the bluff, the ravine grew steeper and the stream narrower.

When they reached a place with jagged, steplike rocks, Libby climbed out on one of them. Between the rocks, the water swirled with a greater current than Libby had ever seen.

"We can jump from here to there," she said, pointing to a rock a short distance away. Beyond that lay another steplike stone, and yet another. "The water isn't deep."

"But it's fast." Jordan sounded doubtful. "If you take a tumble, you shoots right down the whole ravine."

Looking around, he searched for a better way. Along the sides of the stream lay sticks and leaves washed downhill when the stream was higher. Here and there, scattered tree branches lay whitening in the sun. None of them looked large enough to set in place for a bridge.

As Libby studied the rocks again, she heard the call of a crow. "*Caw, caw, caw!*" At first she didn't pay any attention. Then Libby remembered. *The danger signal!*

"*Caw, caw, caw!*"

Libby looked up. Above them, Caleb had reached the ledge and crawled out. Lying on his stomach, he raised an arm, pointing in the direction from which they came.

Palms up, Jordan held out his hands as if asking, "What should we do?"

Caleb pointed to him and Libby, then across the stream. His hand moved quickly, as if telling them to hurry.

"We gots to go," Jordan said. Again he eyed the jagged stones, as if not trusting them. "You first," he said when Libby hesitated. "I stays between you and the catchers."

From the rock on which she stood, Libby made her first jump. From there she leaped to the next flat rock. Beyond was another steplike stone. When she landed safely, Libby glanced back, looking for Jordan. Instead, she saw three people walk out of the woods.

Libby stared at them. The first two were the bullies who had chased Jordan. But the third—

Even from this distance, Libby saw that he was better dressed than the others. Wearing a brown suit and a beaver hat, he had glasses perched halfway down his nose.

A sound escaped Libby's lips. "It's Doctor Fenton!"

As Jordan leaped to the rock beside her, Libby moaned. "I trusted him! He even offered to keep me safe!"

But Jordan gave her no time to talk. "Keep goin', Libby," he warned. "You gots to keep goin'."

Libby's next jump was wobbly. *Fenton! Of all people, it had to be him?* Deep down, Libby felt betrayed.

Trying to push aside her anger, she jumped again. Two more leaps, and she would make it. But suddenly she froze. The next rocks were too far apart.

As she tried to think what to do, Jordan caught up. "Hurry! They's breathing down your back." Using nearby rocks, he leaped past her and landed on the far side of the stream.

With growing terror, she stared at the way Jordan had taken. With her shorter legs the leap was too great.

"Go there!" Jordan pointed downstream to other stones.

Instead, Libby whirled around. Fenton and the two slave catchers hurried toward the ravine.

"I see you!" Fenton shouted. "Stop!"

Libby's heart raged. *He fooled me! He'll take Jordan back into slavery! He'll have proof that Pa hid a runaway slave!*

From the far bank, Jordan again pointed to the stones Libby should take. Instead, panic washed over her. Choosing the nearer path, she leaped.

As Libby fell short, the shock of cold water ripped through her body. When she tried to touch bottom, the current rushed against her, pushing up her feet.

I can swim, Libby thought as the water tore away her shawl. With all her strength, she fought for a handhold. Instead, the current tossed her against a rock.

Suddenly she heard the sharp crack of a large piece of ice giving way. A roaring sound filled her ears.

"Libby!" Jordan shouted. "The ice dam broke!"

18

Jordan's Choice

Libby heard the terror in Jordan's voice. Then a mighty wall of water washed over her. Like a rag doll, she was tossed one way, then another. When she tried to breathe, her mouth filled with water.

With every instinct Libby fought for the surface. As she gasped for air, her shoulder struck a jagged rock. Moments later the water swept her against another stone. This time her leg caught the blow.

Libby's panic grew. *My head. The rocks!*

Reaching out, she tried to shield herself. To catch something. To hang on. But her hands slipped away.

The rocks, she thought again. *They'll knock me out. What can I do?*

With her last bit of strength, Libby managed to lift her arms, clasp her head, stretch out her legs. In the next swirl of water, something changed. As the torrent carried her, Libby shot feet first down the ravine. As if sliding down a stairway, she rode the current.

The rounded tops of stones hit her back. Jagged rocks along

the side tore her arms and shoulders. Her feet struck other rocks, and she almost flipped around.

For one brief instant, Libby saw Jordan running along the stream. In the next moment, he stumbled and was gone. Then the current brought Libby to the end of the ravine. As she felt herself dropping, she screamed. "Help!"

Carried by water, she splashed down into the creek. Pushed under, she fought to the surface. Again the current swept her downstream.

Instinctively Libby raised her arms, tried to swim. But she was numb now. Numb with fear and cold. Too tired to swim.

Her head felt light, her breath gone. Her body started to go limp.

"Libby!"

From far away she heard the cry. Once more Libby fought, stroking down with her hands. Just then she bumped against something.

Struggling to breathe, Libby grabbed hold. Pulled herself up. Gasped for air.

The branches of a fallen cottonwood held her. Relief poured through Libby. *I'm safe!*

Then the branches wavered. The current pushed at Libby, as if trying to sweep her and the tree downstream.

How long? she wondered desperately. *How long can I hang on?*

"Libby!"

Turning her head, she saw Jordan standing in the creek. With water around his waist, he held out a strong branch.

"Grab hold!" he called.

Clinging to the tree with one hand, Libby reached out with the other. Jordan's branch was too far away.

Walking deeper into the water, he called again. "Grab it!"

Again Libby reached out. Still the branch was too far.

Clutching the wood with both hands, Jordan walked still deeper. The icy water reached his shoulders, then touched his chin. Terror filled his eyes as he struggled to hold the branch between them.

Three feet still lay between Libby and the end of the branch. As the current swirled around him, Jordan wavered, almost going down.

In that instant Libby found her feet against the trunk of the cottonwood. With all her strength she pushed herself toward Jordan. When she caught hold of the branch, he stepped back.

"Hang on!" he called, moving back again.

Libby clung to the branch. As the current pounded against her, Jordan drew her toward shore.

When at last Libby's feet touched bottom, the branch guided her in. Only when Libby stumbled onto land did Jordan stop.

Safely above the raging creek, Libby fell onto the ground. With great, long gasps she struggled for breath. Her heart still pounded when she felt the cold air on her wet clothing. Desperate again, Libby pushed herself up and looked around. Through a haze she saw Jordan kneeling on the ground.

His arms stretched high above his head, he gazed up at the sky. "Thank you, Lord! Praise you, Jesus! Hallelujah!"

As if she were still living it, Libby remembered the terror in Jordan's eyes, the water up to his chin. "How did you get here?" Libby asked through chattering teeth. Already she felt chilled to the bone.

"I run with all my might." As though just feeling the cold, Jordon started shaking.

Still unable to take in all that had happened, Libby stared at the bluff above them. Where the ravine emptied into the creek, water poured over straight-up-and-down rocks. *Did I fall that far?*

Then she saw the steep hill next to the rocks. *Jordan ran down that and lived?*

"We gots to move, Libby." Jordan struggled to speak. "We gots to move, no matter what."

Libby's wet clothing clung to her. When she took her first step, she felt bruises in every part of her body. As she looked down, she saw blood oozing from jagged cuts on her arms. But the blood seemed to belong to someone else.

Then Libby remembered. "Where's Caleb?"

Jordan shook his head. His helpless shrug said more than words.

Libby moaned. *Maybe the chunk of ice hit Caleb's head. Maybe he was right in front of that wall of water. Maybe he was washed downstream.*

Forgetting all the times she and Caleb hadn't gotten along, Libby only wanted to be sure he was safe. But her mind felt numb with shock.

Then through a growing haze, Libby saw a boy making his way down the steep hill. Hanging on to small trees and bushes, he dropped rapidly from one level to the next. Still feeling confused, Libby finally realized it was Caleb.

When he reached them, he stared at Libby as though unable to believe what he was seeing. "Are you all right?" he whispered. A strange mixture of fear and relief filled his eyes.

Quick tears welled up, blurring Libby's vision. Caleb had never looked better. As her tears spilled over, he spoke.

"I saw everything from above. I'm mighty glad you're still with us, Libby."

"You too," she answered when she could speak.

Caleb clapped Jordan on the back, helped him to his feet. "Thanks, my friend," Caleb said simply. "I wouldn't have liked the job of telling Libby's pa."

Quickly Caleb glanced around. "C'mon," he told Jordan and Libby. "I found a cave. I'll make a fire."

Taking Libby's hand, Caleb drew her arm across his shoulders. Giving her support, he angled his way up the steep hill. Staying close by, Jordan staggered so he could barely walk. More than once, Caleb waited to encourage him on.

Libby's shoes sloshed with water. As though she were walking on a thousand needles, her feet prickled. But soon the climbing grew worse. Clutching at bushes and small trees, Caleb helped her up, then stretched out his free hand for Jordan.

In the rubble of the limestone hillside, Libby's feet sank in. When she slid and would have fallen, Caleb clung to her hand. Pain shot up Libby's arm. Step by step, her misery grew.

As though looking for patches of grass or flat rocks for footholds, Caleb paused often. Then, tugging and pulling, he drew Libby on. Gradually she felt warmer. When the hill grew even steeper, she started to perspire. Turning around, she looked for Jordan. Climbing not far behind them, he, too, looked warm. Beads of sweat stood out on his forehead.

The moment they reached the cave, Caleb lit a match and checked inside. Then he drew Libby into the darkness. As she started to fall, Caleb caught and lowered her to the ground. Kneeling down, he pulled off her shoes. From the bag on his back, he took out dry clothes.

"Take off your wet clothes and use these," he said. "When you come out, I'll have a fire."

The moment he left, the cold again struck Libby. After her warmth during the climb, the cold air seemed even worse. As it crept into her inner being, Libby fumbled with buttons and fingers too numb to work.

Trembling in every bone of her body, she pulled off her wet clothing. Again she saw the blood on her arms and legs. Yet she couldn't take in what the bruises and cuts meant.

When at last she finished dressing, Libby had only one thought. *Caleb promised a fire!*

Near the entrance of the cave, he had it going. Feeling dazed, Libby sank down next to the flames. Caleb wrapped a dry blanket around her.

Already Jordan huddled as close to the fire as he could get without being burned. Caleb had given him his jacket and cap and every dry piece of clothing he had left.

In spite of the fire, Libby felt she would never be warm again. As her numbness started to wear away, her bruises came alive. Only then did she see the scrape marks on her hands.

Using the small pail he had carried, Caleb was heating a chunk of ice. When the water was hot enough, he poured it into tin cups. The warm liquid flowing down Libby's throat made her feel better, but her teeth still chattered.

Across the fire, Jordan also shook with cold. Seeing him, Libby remembered what he had done. As though living it again,

she saw his terror, the water up to his chin, the branch he held out to her.

"Jordan?" Libby struggled to speak. "You don't know how to swim, do you? You waded out to save me, and you don't know how to swim."

As though it were nothing, Jordan shrugged. But the shrug ended with his whole body shaking.

Watching him, Libby remembered the slave catchers. *Fenton! Not Riggs like we thought.*

"Where are they?" Libby could barely get out the words.

But Caleb understood. "The slave catchers? I hope they're on the other side of the ravine."

Caleb's voice was quieter than usual, as if he still couldn't believe that Libby was alive. "From what your pa said, the creek spreads even wider below where we were. If Fenton and his bullies try to cross the mud flats, they'll find standing water. If they try it the way you did, they'll be in just as much trouble."

Unless the stream slows down. Suddenly Libby knew she was thinking again. "Fenton fooled us." This time Libby's shiver did not come from cold. "He lied. He pretended he was something he wasn't." Libby felt angry now. In spite of her misery, questions plagued her. "Won't the smoke give us away?"

"Take a look!"

As Libby turned in the direction where Caleb pointed, Libby saw the smoke drifting back into the cave.

"There's a crack in the limestone drawing the smoke," Caleb said. "Somewhere back there, it'll escape—away from us." For the first time since Libby's accident, Caleb grinned. "Maybe it's God's protection."

Soon Caleb divided his remaining sandwiches between Jordan and Libby. "That's the last one," he said when they finished eating. "You can't be hungry tomorrow."

"Tomorrow!" Libby exclaimed. "By now we should have found Doctor Sweney. Look at the time we've wasted because of Fenton!"

"But we're this far," Caleb told her. "We still have the hope of getting help for Elsa."

With each minute that passed, Libby discovered another bruise. When she touched her face, she felt dried blood on her cheek.

Taking a clean cloth from his bag, Caleb wet it in the last of the warm water. "Hold still," he said as he knelt down next to Libby. Gently he washed the cut on her cheek.

While melting more ice, he checked her arms. Here, too, she had scrapes and bruises. "Does anything feel broken?" Caleb asked.

When Libby shook her head, he spoke softly. "It's a miracle that you're alive. You know that, don't you?"

Carefully he washed the cuts on her arms, then set her shoes next to the fire. When they started steaming, Caleb took warm soil from near the fire and put it in her shoes.

"Hey! What are you doing?" Libby asked.

"Drying up the insides."

As soon as Libby stopped shaking, she spread out her wet clothes. Deep down, she ached. "I thought we could trust Fenton!"

Libby looked across the fire. "But Jordan knew better."

"I ain't never had no likin' for that man," he muttered.

Libby remembered Jordan's words. She wished she had listened to him. "Do you think Riggs hired Fenton to be a slave catcher?" she asked Caleb.

"I'm sure of it," he answered. "Why else would Fenton have come on the boat when he did?"

It made Libby angry. "We looked so hard for Riggs, and he sent someone else! Or do you think Riggs is still on the *Christina*?"

"We'll find out when we go back," Caleb told her. "Right now it's Fenton and his two slave catchers we worry about."

If they come up the hill—Libby tried to push the thought away. If the slave catchers suddenly appeared, she could barely stand up, let alone run.

Like a guard, Caleb sat on the outer edge of the fire next to the entrance of the cave. As the sun went down behind the bluff towering above them, the temperature dropped. In the gray twilight, Caleb gathered more wood. When he had a good-sized heap, he sat down again.

Jordan also faced the opening of the cave. Though his teeth still chattered, his eyes were watchful.

So the danger isn't past, Libby thought. *They're still wondering. And waiting.*

As twilight deepened into darkness, Caleb often got up and prowled around, watching and listening. When Jordan straightened up as though finally warm, Caleb faced him. "Jordan, is Libby right? You don't know how to swim?"

"I don't know how, but I gots to learn," Jordon said. "What if I need to help my family cross a river to freedom?"

As though still living that frightful moment in the creek, Libby remembered. *Jordon risked his life—everything—to get his freedom. Yet now that he has it, he almost gave his life for me.*

Libby couldn't understand a gift like that. "Jordan," she asked. "How could you wade in to save me when you don't know how to swim?"

"I had to," he told her.

"No, you didn't." The terror in Jordan's face was still real to Libby. "Someone else might have let me drown. What if *you* had drowned?"

"If I did, I was ready."

"Ready for what?" Libby asked.

"Ready to die."

"You knew that you might die to pull me out?" she asked.

"Yes'm. But I didn't think about it." Jordan sounded as if his actions were a surprise, even to himself. "If I had thunk on it, I would have done the same thing."

"Why?" Libby asked.

"For your pa's sake." Jordan grinned. "And for yours."

Libby swallowed against a lump in her throat. Nothing could possibly say what she felt, but she had to try. "I can't thank you enough, Jordan."

He nodded, receiving her words. Yet Libby knew he still didn't think he had done very much.

As the night grew deeper, Libby looked to the darkness beyond the fire, and her fear returned. *What if the slave catchers creep up the hill? In the minute they find us, Jordan loses his freedom.*

"Jordan, how do you stand it?" she asked. "How do you stand knowing that at any moment a slave catcher might find you?"

19

Big Trouble!

*I*n the firelight Jordan glanced beyond the entrance of the cave. When he looked back, his eyes were solemn. "If I was by myself, I couldn't stand it."

By myself. That's it! Deep inside, Libby felt an emptiness that never seemed to go away. Those moments when she could have died still seemed too real.

"I *do* try to do everything by myself," she said softly.

"You needs to know how to be free," Jordan told her. "I has been free for a long time."

Libby felt puzzled. "I thought you just escaped from slavery."

Jordan grinned. "That Riggs. That Old Massa of mine. They just look on the outside. They thinks, 'I own that boy.' But me, I knows better. In here—"

Jordan pointed to his heart. "In here I was free, even when I were a slave. It's Jesus that makes me free, Libby. You gots to let Jesus git you!"

"But how?" Libby whispered. She wanted to pretend that she had all the right answers. Instead, she remembered Ma being strong even when she was afraid. Pa staying calm while Riggs came up the stairs, planning to arrest him. Caleb standing against what he believed was wrong. And Jordan risking everything to save her from drowning.

In that moment there was something Libby knew. She turned to Caleb. "It takes courage to believe in God, doesn't it?"

His gaze meeting hers, Caleb nodded.

"But when you do, God *gives* you courage?" Libby asked. "Is that how it works?"

Again Caleb nodded.

A great sobbing rose in Libby's throat. "Then how do I let Jesus get me?"

In the firelight Caleb leaned forward. "He's already done everything for you, Libby. He wants to give you His love and forgiveness. Just ask for it."

Just ask for it. The words hung between them on the night air.

As Libby bowed her head to pray, tears ran down her cheeks. Yet by the time she finished praying, she felt peaceful deep inside.

❀

The next morning Libby woke to the sound of Caleb putting wood on the fire. Kneeling down next to Jordan, Caleb shook him awake.

"Time for your swimming lesson," he said when Jordan sat up.

"Swimming lesson?" As though forgetting what he'd said the night before, Jordon wiggled closer to the fire. "You foolin' me?"

"Nope! Some time you might need to know how. Like when we go after your family."

Libby shivered as though still feeling the icy water of the creek. "A swimming lesson in April?" The gray light outside the cave told her the sun wasn't yet above the horizon.

"I'll just teach you enough to survive," Caleb promised Jordan. "Now watch."

Holding out his hands, Caleb spread his fingers wide. "If you're scared and push at the water this way, it goes right through your fingers. But if you hold them together—"

Caleb showed him. "You can push down against the water and stay up."

As soon as Jordan held his fingers the right way, Caleb put his hands against Jordan's back. "Lean back like you're lying down in water."

When Jordan obeyed, Caleb told him, "Tip back your head. Breathe deep so your chest fills with air."

When Jordan sat up again, Caleb asked, "Got it?"

Jordan nodded.

"Good!" Caleb exclaimed. "If you really need to know this, you'll be mighty scared."

Several times he asked Jordan to do it again. Always Caleb made sure that Jordan tipped back his head and filled his lungs with air.

As the gray light grew stronger, Libby dumped the dirt from her shoes. Caleb put out the fire. Moving quietly and watching for Fenton and the slave catchers, they picked their way down the bluff. At the bottom they followed the north side of Bullard's Creek.

"If we run into trouble, keep going no matter what," Caleb said.

No matter what? Libby wondered. She dreaded the thought.

With every step she took, Libby wondered if Fenton was behind them. Were he and his men still watching and waiting, ready to follow?

After sitting next to the fire all night, Libby's shoes were dry but stiff. Her back ached and every part of her body felt bruised. Yet somehow she managed to keep up with the boys.

Often Caleb and Jordan glanced around, keeping a close watch. Now and then Jordan sang quietly:

I got wings,
You got wings,
All God's children got wings.

This time Libby felt the words were for her. She remembered

her mother's verse. *You are with me, Jesus! You are my God!*

When at last Libby and the boys entered Red Wing, they followed a string of logs across a marsh. After asking directions, they found Doctor Sweney.

As they told their story, the doctor listened carefully. "What has been done for Elsa?" he asked.

When Caleb explained, the doctor answered, "Good. I'll start right away. Maybe your friend is still alive."

Quickly Doctor Sweney filled his medical bag with needed supplies. "Before you eat, find our mailman, Uncle Dave Hancock. This is the day he makes his weekly trip down to Reads Landing. If he's taking a wagon, maybe you can catch a ride."

All the way back to Reads Landing, Libby and the boys watched for Fenton. In a muddy spot near Bullard's Trading Post, Caleb pointed down. The shoes of three different horses were clearly visible.

"Maybe Fenton got hold of some horses," Caleb said.

"Does that mean he went back to the *Christina*?" Libby asked.

As though wishing he knew, Caleb shrugged. "Maybe. Maybe not," he said. "We'll find out."

❈

When at last they reached the *Christina*, Samson spied them from the top deck and raced down to the gangplank. Wagging his tail until it seemed ready to fall off, he welcomed them back.

"Good dog!" Libby cried, kneeling down to throw her arms around his neck.

As soon as the boys petted Samson, they all bounded up the steps to the texas deck. They found Doctor Sweney outside the door to Libby's room.

"Elsa is still very sick," Doctor Sweney said as he shook Caleb's hand. "Your good directions about drinking a lot of water may be what has kept her alive."

Alive, Libby thought. The gift of life now seemed very precious to her.

❋

From there Libby hurried to her father's cabin. She found Pa in his big rocking chair, looking out the window.

When he saw Libby he jumped up. A warm welcome leaped into his eyes. As Pa opened his arms, Libby walked into them. She couldn't remember ever feeling so glad for his hug.

"You're all right?" he asked. Holding her out at arm's length, Pa studied her face.

Libby met his eyes and nodded. But then Pa saw the scrape on her cheek and the bruises and cuts on her arms and legs. Together they sat down, and she told him the story from beginning to end.

"You're not feeling sick?" he asked finally, and Libby shook her head.

At last she said, "Pa, I understand now. I understand what you believe about God, and I believe the same way."

When Pa gave her another hug, Libby saw the tears in his eyes. One of them slid down his cheek.

❋

The next afternoon Libby stood on the hurricane deck feeling the warmth of the sun. *April 30. Maybe—just maybe, this is the day for the big race!*

Overhead against a cloudless blue sky, smoke billowed out of the tall stacks. From her lookout high on the *Christina*, Libby gazed upstream, hoping for the best.

Even so, she felt uneasy. Going up the stairway the night before, she had looked down to where passengers walked on the boiler deck. For one moment she saw the man she felt sure was Riggs. When she raced down the steps to find out, he was gone.

Ever since, Libby had wondered about him. Wondered, too, about Fenton and his slave catchers. They seemed to have vanished.

Only once since returning from Red Wing had Libby seen Jordan. Then she had noticed his eyes. *He always watches*, she thought. *Jordan wants to know who's behind him.*

"Doctor Sweney would like to get Elsa to Red Wing," Caleb said when he found Libby on the hurricane deck.

Caleb's expression told her that he, too, wanted Elsa in a place that was warm—a room with a wood stove and all that she needed to get well.

"Isn't it good to know how you helped Elsa?" Libby asked softly. "How you told Mrs. Meyer to give Elsa lots of water?"

Then Libby lowered her voice. "I think I saw Riggs." She told Caleb about it, then asked if he knew anything about Fenton.

Caleb shook his head. "He must have offered those slave catchers a big amount of money. They won't just disappear from our lives."

"Good afternoon!" As Pa joined them, Libby saw the warm light in his eyes. He looked as excited as Libby felt.

"Have you heard?" he asked. "Usually there are only ten or twelve boats waiting for the ice to go out. Right now there are *twenty-two*! Not since 1844 has Pepin taken so long to open!"

With their bows nosed into the waterfront and lying only a few feet apart, the boats seemed wedged between each other. On one side of the *Christina* was the *War Eagle*. On the other side, the *Golden State*.

Already the *Christina* had her steam up, ready to go if the ice opened. Farther upstream, along the river's edge, the stretch of water between the bank and the ice had widened. Yet the mass of ice farther upstream still seemed solid.

Then Libby leaned forward. "Is that an opening? A dark space in the ice? Or is it my imagination?" Even as she pointed, the narrow crack of black water widened.

Caleb grinned. "It's what we're waiting for!"

"Here we go!" Pa hurried away.

Moments later the warning bell rang three times. They would start at once.

Bells and whistles filled the air. Eager to see everything, Libby followed Caleb down to the main deck. When he started toward the engine room, Libby trailed behind.

On the *Golden State* and the *Christina*, deckhands worked feverishly. As they tossed their lines aboard, Caleb whirled around and started back to Libby. Looking beyond Caleb, she guessed the reason.

Two tough-looking fellows stood near the door to the engine room. To Libby they seemed familiar. Suddenly she knew who they were. The slave catchers!

Just then one of the bullies stepped into Caleb's path. The other started talking to him. Libby's fists knotted in fear. *Caleb's in big trouble!*

But there was something else. *Is it just a coincidence?* Libby wondered. *Or do the slave catchers know they're blocking the way to Jordan's hiding place?*

20

Race for Life

$\mathcal{F}$illed with panic, Libby turned back to the stairs. *Where's Pa? I've got to find him!*

Just then Jordan bounded down the steps. When he nearly crashed into Libby, she stopped him. "What's wrong?" she asked.

"Fenton!" Jordan pointed behind him.

"Wait!" Libby cried.

"I has to hide!"

Libby felt sure he wanted to reach the secret place in the hold. "You can't," she said. "The slave catchers stopped Caleb!"

Libby peered around the corner. Caleb and one man still stood close to the engine room door, blocking the hatch Libby had found. Like a watch dog, the other slave catcher had moved forward and stood near the door to the cargo space. Beyond that door was the second hatch for Jordan's hiding place.

"They've blocked off your secret place!" Libby warned.

Frantically Jordan looked back up the stairs. "Fenton's after me! I is trapped!"

Just then a whistle tooted. "The *War Eagle!*" Jordan whispered.

The steamboat lay on the side away from where Caleb stood. Crouching down, Jordan kept his head low. Weaving between freight and passengers, he crept across the *Christina's* deck. When he reached the edge, Jordan leaped, landing on the *War Eagle*. In the next instant, he disappeared behind their freight.

Not one second later, Fenton hurried down the stairs. To avoid his questions, Libby quickly walked away. *I can't go to Pa now. Fenton would know what I'm doing.*

Trying to pretend that nothing was wrong, Libby slipped into the crowd at the bow. As the *Christina* steamed upriver, the *War Eagle* slipped into place beside her.

A few minutes later Caleb joined Libby. Facing forward with his back to the passengers, he spoke in a low voice. "Did you see what happened?"

"Worse." Libby also looked straight ahead. "Fenton was after Jordan."

"So they all came back! They probably thought their best bet was to keep an eye on the *Christina*. They were right."

Caleb sounded as though he were talking about the weather. But Libby knew better. He, too, was deeply concerned.

"And they stayed out of our way till now," Libby said. "They must have thought this was a good time to capture Jordan." Libby told Caleb what had happened to Jordan.

"He's on the *War Eagle*?" Caleb spoke just as quietly.

"I saw him make the leap. I think he's somewhere between those piles of freight."

"And Fenton?" Caleb asked. "What happened to him?"

"I don't think he knows where Jordan went," Libby said. "What will Jordan do?"

"Pretend he's a deckhand."

"And work as though he belongs on the *War Eagle*?"

"That's what I'd do."

"Caleb, do you always think about what you'd do? Do you always plan ahead?"

Caleb grinned. "With you on board, I might have to stop trying. And we still don't know if Riggs is here."

As the *Christina* reached Lake Pepin, Libby tried to see every-thing. Sure enough, there was a narrow channel of black water.

Three other paddle-wheelers were ahead of them. As they steamed farther into the lake, Libby saw giant blocks of shifting, crumbling ice. When the lane they had entered seemed to widen, she felt relieved.

Soon the *War Eagle* passed the *Hamburg* and the *Sam Young*. As the *Christina* kept up to the *War Eagle*, the other boats fell behind.

Turning, Libby watched the steamboats that followed them. From their time of waiting at Reads Landing, she recognized many of them. The *Golden State* was coming up fast. When she passed the *Christina*, Libby moaned. "Two ahead of us now."

"Just wait," Caleb told her. "It's a long race yet."

As Libby and Caleb watched, the *Golden State* kept gaining on the *War Eagle*. Libby tried to remember Caleb's words, but she found it hard.

Then a large cake of ice floated by, close to the *Christina*'s wooden hull. Seeing the ice, Libby felt uneasy. Around them the wind and current pushed against the thick, jagged blocks.

Soon shifting ice started to fill the narrow lane of black water. Huge chunks bumped against the *Christina*, jolting the boat. Libby felt glad that Elsa no longer made her bed close to the edge of the deck.

When the sound of bumping ice grew stronger, Libby's un-easiness grew. When she faced into the wind, she felt sure it had picked up.

"I don't like it," Caleb said.

Libby knew the great chunks of ice could break a hole in the *Christina*'s hull. *Is that why there aren't any runaway slaves in the hiding place?* Libby didn't know if the *Christina* brought fugitives this far north. Yet the first run to St. Paul would be extra dangerous for anyone down in the hull.

Looking back again, Libby saw more boats in their wake. The *Galena*, the *Falls City*, and half a dozen others.

"C'mon," Caleb said as the wind grew stronger. "We better go up to your pa's cabin."

From there they watched the ice start to layer. One huge block slid on top of another. Frightened now, Libby watched the ice build up. Small peaks appeared here and there across the wide lake.

Suddenly a gust of wind caught the drifting ice. Close behind the *Christina*, the ice slammed into the *Falls City*, forcing the steamboat up on shore. Her hull crushed like an eggshell, the *Falls City* keeled on one side.

Libby gasped in terror. "What happened to the people?"

"They'll be all right," Caleb said. "Part of the boat is on land. But the boat looks like a total wreck."

As they watched, passengers scrambled up a stairway. Within minutes the main deck of the *Falls City* disappeared under water. On the tilting upper decks, people clung to whatever would hold them until someone on land rescued them.

With ice shifting all around her, the *Christina* poured on even more steam, making a run for it. Through the long hours of the passage through Lake Pepin, Libby stood in Pa's cabin with Caleb and Samson beside her.

Ahead of them, the *Golden State* and the *War Eagle* stayed only a short distance apart. Once Libby felt sure she saw Jordan working on the *War Eagle*'s deck.

At Wacouta, the head of Lake Pepin, the *Christina* finally steamed into safer waters. Libby felt weak with relief to see the last of the ice.

By now the *Golden State* had fallen back, but Captain Laughton's boat, the *Galena*, had crept up. Though the *War Eagle* stayed in the lead, the *Galena* was closing in.

"We're getting close to Red Wing," Caleb told Libby shortly after dark. Together they walked back to stand outside her room.

Doctor Sweney had allowed no one but Mrs. Meyer to see Elsa. Now Libby felt unwilling to have her friend leave without saying goodbye. But Doctor Sweney expected Libby and Caleb to stand at a safe distance.

As Libby watched, the doctor stretched a blanket between two poles to make a stretcher. When Elsa was safely settled, two deckhands picked up the stretcher.

"Goodbye, Elsa," Caleb called as the men headed for the stairs.

Elsa raised a hand. " 'Bye, Caleb." Her pale face seemed the color of her white-blond hair.

Libby wanted to rush forward to hug her. To tell her, "Be sure and get well." Instead she called out, "Auf wiedersehen!"

At the sound of her voice, Elsa tried to lift her head. The shadow of a smile crossed her face. "Auf wiedersehen, Libby," she said softly. "I love you."

Tears welled up in Libby's eyes. "I love *you*, my friend!"

Doctor Sweney went first, walking ahead of the stretcher down the steps, then turning to make sure Elsa was safe. Moving as if she were glass, the deckhands carried her from the texas and hurricane decks to the boiler, then the main deck. Elsa's mother followed close behind. Keeping their distance, Libby and Caleb followed her.

As the *Christina* nosed into the Red Wing waterfront, Doctor Sweney gave his orders. When the gangplank went out, he turned to Libby and Caleb.

"Elsa will get well," he said, as though wanting to give them hope.

A moment later he and Mrs. Meyer, Elsa, and their few belongings were gone.

❋

With lightning speed the deckhands unloaded everything else bound for Red Wing. Again the *Christina* put out, once more racing to St. Paul.

Above Red Wing, a full moon rose over the water. Standing at the bow on the main deck, Libby watched the golden pathway across the river. Samson stood beside her, his great tail thumping against her.

Ahead of them, the *War Eagle* and the *Galena* were neck and neck. Around the *Christina* were a dozen other boats. Osborne, the chief engineer, poured on steam. One by one, the other boats fell away, and the distance between the *Christina* and the lead boats grew less.

"We're catching up!" Libby told Caleb as he came to stand beside her.

As though she could push the *Christina* ahead, Libby leaned into the wind. If only they could overtake the *War Eagle* and the *Galena*. If only Pa could win first place. Just the honor would bring him even more business!

Then, as Libby wished, it seemed to happen. Instead of a great leap forward, the *Christina* crept gradually ahead. Inch by inch, she moved up on the *War Eagle*'s starboard side. As the bow of the *Christina* came even with the stern of the *War Eagle*, moonlight fell on the small deck in back of the cargo space.

Libby grabbed Caleb's arm. "There's Jordan on the deck!"

"He's awfully close to the edge," Caleb answered. "If the boat jerks, he's in trouble."

Standing on tiptoes, Libby tried to see. "He and a deckhand are tying a rope."

A loud cry cut off Libby's words. "I see him!"

Libby looked up. On the boiler deck above them, Fenton stood at the railing. His angry voice shouted across the water. "I see you, boy! I'll catch you yet!"

Startled, Jordan looked toward Fenton. As the *War Eagle* took a burst of speed, Jordan lost his balance. His arms beat the air. Then he tumbled into the water.

Fear clutched Libby's heart. "Jordan can't swim!"

"Man overboard!" came the cry from the *War Eagle*.

"Man overboard!" Caleb called out.

On both boats warning bells jangled. Paddle wheels stopped.

Libby groaned. "After all that's happened, what if Jordan drowns? What about his family?"

Caleb shook his head. His lips moved as if he were praying, but Libby heard no sound.

"Can he ever remember what you taught him?"

Caleb looked grim. "It seems impossible. But Jordan thinks fast in an emergency."

Seconds later, his head appeared in the water. On the *War Eagle*, deckhands raced to drop their yawl. Soon the small boat headed toward Jordan.

"They'll never make it!" Caleb's voice was filled with dread. "They're too far away from him!"

But the *Christina* was closer to Jordan. In that moment Libby remembered her dog. *Newfoundlands. Bred for rescuing men at sea.*

"Samson!" Libby commanded. She pointed toward Jordan. "Get him!"

In the next instant, the dog jumped up on a crate. His front paws together, he leaped into the river. As water splashed around him, all but Samson's head and shoulders disappeared. A dark shape against the moonlit water, the dog swam straight for Jordan.

Straining forward, Libby kept her gaze on Jordan's head. Suddenly she lost sight of him.

"Where *is* he?" she cried. "I can't see Jordon!"

Still paddling a straight line, Samson kept on. Moments later Jordan surfaced. In spite of the icy water, he tipped back his head. Just barely, Libby saw his neck and shoulders.

"He remembers!" she cried. "Jordan remembers what you taught him!"

With strong, sure strokes, the deckhands from the *War Eagle* raced toward Jordan. Minute by minute, the distance between them narrowed, but Samson was still closer to Jordan.

As time seemed to stand still, his head bobbed up and down. Just before Samson reached him, Jordan slipped beneath the surface again.

Caleb groaned. Then Samson disappeared.

"Where are they?" Libby cried out.

Then she spotted Samson. Grasping Jordan's upper arm and shoulder in his mouth, the dog lifted Jordan's head above water.

Jordan's arms thrashed as he fought against Samson. As the dog hung on, Jordan seemed to realize he was trying to help. Suddenly Jordan stopped struggling.

When he clutched the dog's tail, Samson turned toward the

Christina. The yawl turned with them. Staying close by, the deck-hands followed, making sure Jordan was safe.

As Samson brought Jordan alongside the *Christina,* Libby and Caleb rushed over. Reaching out, Caleb and a deckhand grabbed hold of Jordan. More deckhands helped Samson on board. Then a great cheer went up.

A quick whistle from the *Christina* told the *War Eagle* that all was well. Moments later the *Christina*'s paddle wheels and engines started. As Caleb drew Jordan into the furnace room to change and warm up, the *Christina* again poured on steam.

Just then Libby remembered Fenton. Looking up, she saw that he still stood at the railing on the boiler deck. When the moon lit his face, Libby felt sure she knew his angry thoughts.

He knows he can't take Jordan now. Not with all these people who wanted him rescued.

But there was one thing Libby knew. *Fenton will wait for a better time.*

21

The Winner!

*N*ext to the stove used by the deckers, Libby rubbed Samson with towels. "Good dog!" she told him again and again. Someone had passed the word to Granny, for she brought a special bone.

When Libby once more went out on the main deck, she found Caleb. As if having no more than the usual interest in Jordan, he stood at the bow. But Caleb's eyes were watchful, as though still looking for Riggs. Now and then his gaze flipped up to where Fenton stood.

As they drew close to St. Paul, Libby stood beside Caleb. The full moon still lit a pathway across the water. Though nearly two o'clock in the morning, the decks were full of people watching to see who won the race.

Just then a man crowded close—too close. His cane bumped Libby's bruised leg. Looking down, she saw that the cane had a handle with a gold head. In the seconds it took to look up, Libby's heart pounded.

The short, slender man next to her wore an expensive-looking coat. His beaver hat protected him against the damp night air.

When he turned toward Libby, she saw his blue eyes. Instead of being cold and mean, they looked kind.

Then Libby saw the man's mouth. Above his upper lip the skin was red, as though still healing from the glue that held a mustache. But there were no evil lines between his nose and the outer corners of his lips.

As Libby nudged Caleb with her elbow, the man tipped his hat. "Excuse me, Miss," he said. "I'm sorry about my cane. I hope I didn't hurt you."

Libby smiled. "You didn't hurt me at all," she said. *It's not Riggs!* she thought.

When Libby turned back to Caleb, she saw that he was listening. Without speaking, they waited until the man walked away. "We spent so much time looking for Riggs, we didn't catch on to Fenton," Libby said with regret.

Caleb grinned. "But you're learning fast, Libby."

"Fast enough to—" Libby stopped, afraid to speak the words aloud with so many people close by. *To help with the Underground Railroad*, she thought.

But Caleb understood. "Maybe," he said.

It still bothered Libby. "Do you trust me, Caleb?"

For a moment he thought about it. "I think so."

"Don't I have enough courage?"

This time Caleb answered at once. "You have more than enough courage, Libby. And you get it from the right Person."

Deep inside, Libby felt grateful. Yet she still needed to understand. "So why don't you want me to—"

Libby paused. Again she needed to be careful. *To be a part of the Underground Railroad.* Aloud she said, "Why are you afraid to let me try?"

In the moonlight Caleb's blue eyes were darker than usual. Now they were serious instead of filled with fun. As his gaze met Libby's, he spoke softly. "I'm afraid that something will happen to you."

"That's *all*?" Libby asked.

"Well, isn't that enough?"

"Nothing will happen to me!" As her spirit soared, Libby tossed her head, and her red curls swung about her shoulders. "Unless a bear wants my sandwich. Or an ice dam gives way."

Caleb grinned. "Or you go snooping around a boat in the middle of the night." He lowered his voice still more. "We're ready now," he whispered. "When we go back down the river, Jordan knows exactly how he can help his family escape. His plan sounds as safe as something like that can be. And he's figured out what you and I can do."

"I can help?" Libby asked, startled.

Before Caleb could answer, Jordan came up behind him. In dry clothes again, he wore a sweater and Caleb's warmest jacket. When Jordan tried to talk, his teeth chattered, but Libby understood what he was saying. "If you hadn't sent that dog of yours, I'd be hearin' them angels sing!"

In spite of what had happened, Jordan's eyes glowed, as if knowing a miracle had taken place. "Libby, I ain't able to thank you enough."

"You don't have to say a word," she answered. "Don't forget what you did for me!"

Libby remembered Caleb's words after her near drowning. Now it was her turn to say them. "I'm mighty glad you're still with us, Jordan."

"Me too." In the midst of his shivers Jordan grinned. "I can't be a Moses for my people till I knows how to cross the water."

Just then from farther upstream, they heard the tooting of whistles. Church bells rang, and a cannon sounded.

"It's the welcome in St. Paul," Caleb said.

"A cannon at two o'clock in the morning?" Libby asked. Looking up, she saw that Pa had joined them. "Did the *Galena* win?"

"From here it looks that way. The *War Eagle* can't be more than fifteen minutes behind. Captain Kingman will be second."

Libby felt disappointed for Pa. "What fun it would have been to be first. I wish you could have won."

"No wasted wishes," Pa told her. He looked toward Jordan.

"A person's life is worth more than a free wharf for the season. The *War Eagle*'s captain knows that. So do I."

Pa's honest eyes told Libby that he meant every word. Turning to Caleb, Captain Norstad lowered his voice. "You know what to do," he warned. "Even in Minnesota Territory—"

Libby's thoughts finished the sentence. *Even here, Fenton has the lawful right to capture Jordan. To bring him back into slavery.*

Caleb nodded. "As soon as we reach St. Paul, sir."

"Jordan?" Pa asked.

"I'll stick with Caleb like fleas on a dog's back."

When Pa slipped away, he shook one hand here, another there. Then he moved close to where the gangplank would go down.

As the *Christina* put into St. Paul, passengers pushed toward her bow. In the crowd on the boat, Libby saw Fenton trying to reach Jordan. Yet when the *Christina* reached the landing, Caleb and Jordan were ready. While Pa talked to passengers, using them to block Fenton's way, the two boys hurried down the gangplank.

The moment they reached the riverbank, Caleb started running. Jordan was right behind. Dodging around freight and people, they made their escape.

Without moving Libby waited, hoping for another view. As Caleb started up the bluff above the landing, Libby thought she saw his blond hair in the moonlight. Yes, that was him with Jordan close behind. Then both of them disappeared into the darkness.

Tomorrow I'll see St. Paul, Libby promised herself. *And I'll see Caleb.* Turning away, she smiled.

A Note From Lois

Thanks to each of you who have written to tell me how much you like the Northwoods Adventures and the first Riverboat Adventure. I love to hear from my readers and feel as though we've become friends through books.

If you would like to receive my newsletter, let me know by writing to:

Lois Walfrid Johnson
Bethany House Publishers
11300 Hampshire Ave. S.
Minneapolis, MN 55438

Please be sure to include *a stamp* on an envelope *addressed to yourself*.

Acknowledgments

Do you know how it feels to desperately want to win something?

Everyone loves a winner, and the stakes for the 1857 race were high. All winter long, the people of St. Paul had waited for the first steamboat to bring passengers, supplies, and news from the outside world. The first captain who passed through Lake Pepin to open the shipping season would be a hero. He would receive both honors and a sizable reward—free use of the St. Paul wharf throughout the season.

History tells us that the *Galena* was the winner, but I vote for the *War Eagle*. In a time when not all steamboat captains stopped for a person who fell overboard, Captain Kingman's choice to put out a yawl was unusual. His act of mercy probably cost him the race, for the *War Eagle* came in second, just fifteen minutes after the *Galena*. Yet even now, a century and a half later, we know that Captain Kingman cared more about one man's life than about personal wealth and honor.

If you're in the St. Louis area, you'll find some special places to visit. The Jefferson National Expansion Memorial offers excellent museums under the Arch and in what is now called the

Old Courthouse. Those who want to know more about Dred Scott will appreciate the display on the first floor of the Old Courthouse. Because of an architectural flaw that threatened the ceiling, the courtroom used for Scott's first two trials was changed in 1855. A second-floor courtroom has been restored to its nineteenth-century appearance and looks like the one used for Scott's trials in 1847 and 1850.

Today we're sensitive about how we refer to people of color. In this book and others in The Riverboat Adventures series, I've tried to give the language used in the 1850s in order to create a real and historically accurate picture.

As always, I'm deeply grateful to those who help me write a book. With this novel Chuck Peterson of Grantsburg, Wisconsin, has especially blessed me with his sense of story and his willingness to provide information and read portions of the manuscript. Thanks, too, Chuck, for the time you and Lori gave in showing Roy and me your boyhood haunts in the Red Wing area.

Robert L. Miller, curator of the *George M. Verity*, the Keokuk River Museum at Victory Park in Keokuk, Iowa, also has a sense of what is needed to create a story. In this National Historic Landmark I first began to feel what it was like to live on a riverboat. Since then, Bob has generously given of his wisdom and resources. His patience in reading portions of the manuscript and answering my countless questions is amazing!

Other people gave me exactly the right help at just the moment I needed it: Emily Miller, librarian, Missouri Historical Society Library and Research Center, St. Louis, Missouri; Charlene Gill, president, Alton Area Historical Society, Alton, Illinois; Roberta Hagood, author and historian, Hannibal, Missouri; Emma Lee Lahmeyer Hill, Keokuk Public Library, Keokuk, Iowa; Susie Guest, library assistant, Burlington Free Public Library; and *The Hawk Eye*, Iowa's oldest newspaper, also in Burlington.

Thanks to the librarians at the Wabasha, Minnesota, Public Library and to Charlie McDonald and the Wabasha County Historical Museum at Reads Landing, Minnesota. In the Red Wing, Minnesota, area, my gratitude to Char Henn, present curator;

Mary Maronde, director; Jean Chesley, retired director; and Orville Olson, former curator of the Goodhue County Historical Society. I'm also grateful to Adeline Deden, Evelyn Sweasy, Kathryn Morrow, and the Red Wing Public Library for their help.

Thanks to Tom Benson, Hartland, Minnesota, who calls like a crow and gets the owls to answer; Norma Robinson, president, Newfoundland Dog Club of the Greater Twin Cities, Eagan, Minnesota; Dr. William Young of the River Valley Medical Center, St. Croix Falls, Wisconsin; the librarians at the Grantsburg Public Library in Grantsburg, Wisconsin; and to Charlotte Adelsperger, Overland Park, Kansas, who tells me to feed my characters.

In St. Paul, Minnesota, thanks to the Minnesota Historical Society for their Minnesota History Center and especially their research facilities. Thanks to the St. Paul *Pioneer Press* for *The Daily Pioneer* and *Democrat* newspapers.

I am grateful to the *Arabia* Steamboat Museum in Kansas City, Missouri, for its massive undertaking in bringing up and restoring an 1856 cargo that sank on the Missouri River. Thanks to all who have been involved in this exciting project and especially to Greg Hawley and David Hawley for answering my questions.

My gratitude to Maurice J. Montgomery, curator/archivist of the Rock County Historical Society for his tour of the Tallman House in Janesville, Wisconsin. I also appreciate Judy Scheehle and the Milton House, an authentic stop on the Underground Railroad in Milton, Wisconsin.

Special thanks to the entire Bethany House team: my artist, Andrea Jorgenson, for her cover and story illustrations; Toni Auble for her side-wheeler diagram; and Barbara Lilland and Rochelle Glöege for their editing and ongoing encouragement.

As an author, I value all my editors, but I've worked with one person more than any other. A gifted author and editorial director, Ron Klug has now edited sixteen of my books. Always he does so with grace and style, offering a sensitive understanding of how to improve what I've begun. With this novel, I owe him even more gratitude than usual because of his wise counsel and his vision for the meaning of courage. Thanks, too, Ron, for your and Lyn's friendship.

For many years more people than I can name have offered quiet, daily encouragement for me to continue writing. I never take you, nor your time and support, for granted. Bless you!

Every now and then, you, my special readers, address a letter to both my husband, Roy, and me. It's fun when I see that, for I know you understand how much Roy has helped me with the writing of each book. As always, my gratitude to you, Roy, for your love and wisdom, for being my terrific husband, and for the person you are to our children and grandchildren. You've been a dad just like Libby's Pa. Thanks, also, to my own dad, Alvar Walfrid, for being a father I deeply love and respect.